Praise for

Into the Vortex

"Too many books written for young adults seem to deal in hopelessness, and so it is very refreshing to read a gripping and uplifting adventure about 12-year-old Kayden Barrett's resilience in the face of adversity. Author John Poidevant's debut is sure to make him a must-read in middle schools everywhere."

—DANNY BRASSELL, PhD, internationally acclaimed speaker, bestselling author of sixteen books and founder of lazyreaders.com

"*Into the Vortex* conveys a key message for today's youth, 'What is right with you is more important than anything that might be wrong.' The story is a message of hope. A message of resilience. A message that everyone needs to hear and believe. The author understands resilience. He lived it. He passed it on to others, including me. That is a legacy of resilience worthy of this story. Let him pass it on to you."

—KAREN G. GRIFFITH, PhD, author of
*Building Resiliency: A Non-Thematic Small Group
Approach and Creative Small Groups: Ready to Use Lessons*

"Encapsulating the key components of social and emotional learning, *Into the Vortex* is a rapid-paced adventure that engrosses multi-aged readers from its inception. The protagonist's journey toward healing touches on themes faced by so many youth today: fear, anxiety and depression, and the crucial relationship and resiliency skills that can make us stronger. Dr. Poidevant's tale draws upon decades of experience in youth mental health, and his life lessons are practical, relatable, and filled with a message of unsinkable hope. A must-have for school counselors for book clubs or small group lessons!"

—SUSANNA M. BROOKS, MA, M.Ed.,
school counselor, Cherokee County School District

"Over my four decades of navigating challenging whitewater rapids, including winning America's first ever Olympic gold medal in whitewater slalom with my canoe partner, Scott Strausbaugh, I have frequently called 'The River' my best life coach. In his new book, *Into the Vortex*, John wonderfully captures the spirit of the river as a teacher and guide in a way that will engage and inspire young people to work with challenge and fear in pursuit of a good life bound by nature, positive relationships, continual learning, and the power of resilience."

—JOE JACOBI, Olympic gold medalist for whitewater slalom,
Paddler of the Century by *Paddler Magazine*, Performance Coach

"*Into the Vortex* is a gift—a riveting story full of truth, wisdom, and hope, offering the tools of resiliency to youth, parents, educators, and helping professionals in a COVID world. It ought to be required reading for every student, to help them prepare for or recover from life's challenges, and to encourage friends in need."

—REV. JONATHAN HARTZER,
Anglican priest and pastoral counselor, Midland, TX

"*Into the Vortex* is an inspiring story of grit and resilience, one that will suck you in and keep you spiraling until the end. The strong underlying message of hope is timely in our world today, especially for our children. The author also provides numerous learning activities at the end of the book that allow teachers, counselors, students, and parents to gain a greater understanding of the importance of resiliency. *Into the Vortex* is an ideal fit with social emotional learning and promotes self-awareness, building relationships, and responsible decision-making."

—KIM HAGOOD, principal of Carmel Elementary, Cherokee County School District

"*Into the Vortex* is a fast paced read with a powerful message of inner resiliency that should be required reading for all children entering middle school. As a former middle and high school basketball coach I have seen firsthand the real challenges students face as they transition from grade to grade. Kayden Barrett's story of mental toughness is inspiring, victorious and a must read for anyone facing adversity or loss in their life. Dr. Poidevant has simply and effectively mapped the course for rediscovering and rebuilding the resiliency that lies within every one of us."

—BART CHRISTIAN, author of the Simple Solutions book series and nationally recognized education speaker

"John Poidevant has taken his life's work and created an inspiring novel designed to impart resiliency and strength in the worst of situations. *Into the Vortex* provides a strong message of hope, optimism, and redemption. It is a timely read and one that clearly conveys resiliency in action."

—LES CONLEY, retired principal, coach, and teacher, Cherokee County School District

"Using his skill as a gifted writer, Dr. Poidevant is able to envelop the reader in an adventure that both frightens and gives hope. In a time of great anxiety, he offers a sure path for the generations to come. His vast clinical experience has culminated in this great gift."

—CHARLES R. COOLEY, MD, author of *Reindeer Magic* and
president, Kavik Publishing

"In a world filled with mixed social and emotional messages directed at our young teens and adults, it is amazing to read an outstanding book designed to uplift emotional fortitude and promote resiliency! Author John Poidevant has lived a life of serving students who are in need of support and guidance, and his novel reflects those same intentional efforts with his strong message of hope, courage, and determination in the face of adversity. Our young people need more works of literature like *Into the Vortex!*"

—DR. DEBRA MURDOCK, chief operations officer,
Cherokee County School District

Student Endorsements:

"I lost my dad suddenly to cancer when I was 10 years old. About eight months later, I was invited to read *Into the Vortex* with a group of my classmates and discuss the story with the author, Dr. Poidevant. Having been through the loss of a parent, like Kayden Barrett, I found many of the experiences in the book to be like mine. The story gave me hope that things will get better and that I have support systems I can count on at school and at home. It also made me realize that I am more resilient than I thought I was and that I will continue to get stronger."

—EMILY C. SMITH, eleven years old,
Georgia middle school student

"*Into the Vortex* conveys the point to not take life for granted. The book is a great example for young people who have ever experienced a challenging life event. For me, it was early in my life. I have experienced some challenging health issues. Although my health issues and hospital stays were hard, my love, passion, and drive for my sport continues. I have found that my perseverance through those health challenges have made me a better athlete, and hopefully set me up to deal with adversity into adulthood. I have enjoyed the opportunity to read this book."

—ANNA GRESHAM, thirteen years old,
Georgia middle school student

Into the Vortex

a tale of resiliency

John Poidevant

RIVER GROVE
B O O K S

Published by River Grove Books
Austin, TX
www.rivergrovebooks.com

Distributed by River Grove Books

Design and composition by Greenleaf Book Group
Cover design by Greenleaf Book Group
Cover Image: Cave Sunray 3D, used under license from Shutterstock.com.
Interior Images: Whirlpool in the blue water view from above;
Aerial view of river and park illustration; Man in canoe; used under
license from Shutterstock.com.

For permission to reproduce copyrighted material, grateful acknowledgment is made to the following:
"Wreckage" by Nikita Gill. Copyright (c) by Nikita Gill. Reproduced by permission of David Higham Associates Ltd. All rights reserved.

Publisher's Cataloging-in-Publication data is available.

Print ISBN: 978-1-63299-401-1

eBook ISBN: 978-1-63299-402-8

First Edition

This book is dedicated to five remarkable individuals who supported and encouraged me down the path of life:

My wife, *JoAnne*, for her unwavering love, support, and encouragement. She is also the most resilient person I know.

My parents, *A.L.* and *Anne Poidevant*, for believing in me, even when I tested the waters and battled my own vortex.

Mike Barrett, football and wrestling coach at The Bolles School, who served as a positive role model to me and countless other students during their formative years.

Dr. Thomas Renfro, my "second father," whose faith, inspiration, and generosity made this book possible.

*One way to get the most out of life is to
look upon it as an adventure.*

—William Feather

Prologue

The story you are about to read is about hope and resiliency. Kayden Barrett is a twelve-year-old boy who has faced the greatest challenges in life. His world has been turned upside down by a series of uncontrollable events. Ultimately, Kayden must make decisions that will impact his life forever.

Kayden's life has been traumatic, leaving him raw and vulnerable at one of its most challenging stages: middle school. For him, grief has been a frequent companion and has led to far more questions than answers. To make matters worse, for the first time ever, he does not look forward to going to school. The reason is simple, yet it poses a complex problem. A bully has entered his life, creating uncertainty and fear. Sadly, Kayden's main source of strength is no longer available, and he must find other ways to survive seventh grade.

Kayden's journey toward healing is difficult, painful, and full of setbacks, but he discovers a powerful force that helps him. His experiences in nature on free-flowing rivers allow him to refocus. His body and mind become balanced and whole. He refers to this as his "hydrotherapy," and he pursues it at every opportunity. The chance to experience a free-flowing river with beautiful scenery in the company of people he likes is healing. Ultimately, Kayden's journey on the Opa River changes his life forever.

To help you understand the events that take place on the river, a few key terms are defined and illustrated here.

Vortex: a whirling mass of water that forms a central cavity into which suction draws floating objects, as in a whirlpool.

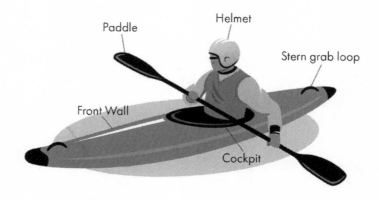

Kayak: a small, narrow watercraft propelled by a double-bladed paddle.

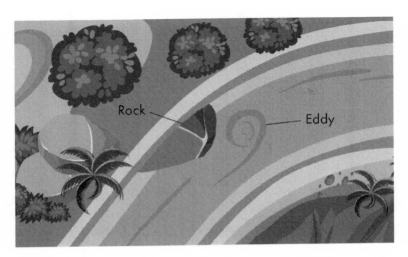

Rock

Eddy

Eddy: A relatively calm spot in a river. An eddy is formed when a current flows around an obstacle and water flows back upstream to fill in the space left by the deflected current. The current in eddies flows upstream. Eddies are great for resting, getting out of a downstream current, and getting out of the river to scout.

Chapter 1

"Once you choose hope, anything is possible!"

—Christopher Reeve

Kayden Barrett awoke at three o'clock on the morning of the kayaking trip. His mind raced with different scenarios he might encounter on the river. After tossing and turning for an hour, he fell back into a deep sleep. He woke up at his usual time, seven o'clock, and placed his feet on the floor. Outside light streaming in the window penetrated the darkness in the bedroom and reflected off his favorite picture: him and his dad on their first paddling trip. The image brought a soft smile to his face followed by a wrenching sensation in his stomach. The tears came quickly and flowed down his cheeks. He quickly wiped most of them away. It had been four years since his dad had died.

Kayden turned his head in the direction of footsteps coming up the stairs. He knew the sound well. He glanced toward the door as Hobie, his five-year-old rescue pup, trotted in toward him. A smile quickly returned to Kayden's face as Hobie snuggled his head into Kayden's lap. Holding Hobie tight, Kayden nestled his face into the fur on the top of the dog's head. It absorbed the last tear on his cheek.

The bond between boy and dog was strong, and it had helped Kayden through the darkest time of his life. Kayden and his dad had picked Hobie out together from the county animal shelter. The director of the shelter had described Hobie as a "*summa* dog," a mixed breed, "*summa* this and *summa* that." Hobie appeared to be a mix of golden retriever and something else. Kayden wasn't sure what else, and it didn't matter. In Kayden's eyes, he was the perfect dog. Hobie stayed by him almost everywhere he went, even the bathroom. Kayden had not taken his canine friend on a river trip yet. He hoped to one day.

Kayden heard sounds in the kitchen, pans being retrieved from a cabinet. This was a welcome and familiar sound on Saturday mornings. Soon his mom's voice channeled up the stairwell.

"Kayden, your breakfast is almost ready," she called. "Come on down!"

As Kayden packed his clothes in a duffel, he noted the distinct aroma of bacon slowly filling his room. This was a tradition on the morning of every paddling trip. Mrs. Barrett would cook a full breakfast for Kayden, usually pancakes and bacon. Paddling trips required energy, and Mrs. Barrett enjoyed sending her son off with a full stomach. Kayden finished packing his duffel bag and rolled the top tight. "I'm coming, Mom," he called back to her. "Be right down."

After checking his gear and making sure he had a change of warm clothes, Kayden grabbed his bag and gently slid it down the steps. He enjoyed watching the bag bounce its way down. For some odd reason, it always landed in the same spot. On his way to the kitchen, he made sure to move the bag to the rug by the front door. He did not want to forget it, again. Long drives in wet clothes were not fun. Kayden had learned this the hard way.

The blueberry pancakes were cooked to perfection, golden brown. He grabbed his plate and selected three of the biggest ones in the stack, leaving plenty of space for bacon. After dousing them with butter and maple syrup, Kayden devoured his breakfast. A large mug of hot chocolate and a glass of milk followed. Mrs. Barrett was shocked at how much food Kayden could eat, especially before an all-day adventure. Breakfast had always been a special time for them, and it had become even more so after Mr. Barrett's passing. Kayden was a morning person and liked to talk. His mom liked to listen.

Mrs. Barrett had been a single parent for four years now. The adjustment had been hard. She had started a new job at the hospital three years earlier and liked her work. She had a degree in nursing but had decided to stay home after Kayden was born. This was her first real job, and it was a good fit. She enjoyed helping others. However, weekday mornings seemed like a mad rush. Kayden had to get ready for school while she rushed about preparing for her day at the hospital.

Mrs. Barrett heard a jeep pull up in the driveway and glanced out the window. "Better hurry, Kayden. Ms. Sullivan and her dad are here. Make sure you have all of your gear."

Kayden put his plate in the sink and hugged his mom. "Thanks for the pancakes, Mom. I'll see you this evening," he said. "Yeah, I know; be careful." He kissed her on the cheek.

Mrs. Barrett held her son tight, her hug lasting a few seconds longer than usual.

Kayden grabbed his gear on the way out and slid into the back seat behind Jo Sullivan and her dad. "Good morning, Jo," he said, holding some cash toward the front passenger seat. "Before I forget, here's some gas money my mom wanted me to give you."

Jo took the money and put it in the console, then turned her head toward him. "Kayden, this is my dad," she said. "He's our shuttle driver today. He'll leave my jeep at the takeout on the river, and my mom will pick him up. My parents are boaters too, but *their* boat has a big sail."

Mr. Sullivan turned and nodded toward Kayden. "Good to meet you," he said. "Jo told me about you. Don't worry, good things!" Jo had described Kayden to her dad as "an old soul," wise beyond his years. But, like most twelve-year-old boys, he sometimes struggled with decisions. Jo liked that Kayden had a hopeful manner about him, even after his dad had died.

Kayden was surprised to see that Jo's jeep had a five-speed manual transmission. Her dad slid the gearshift forward and slowly eased off of the clutch. The morning air was cool, and a gentle breeze came in through the sunroof. The Opa River was an hour's drive from his house, and Kayden had been looking forward to this trip for a long time.

Kayden had met Jo a year earlier at the lake by his house. She was part of the local paddling club Kayden and his dad had joined six years before. She was an experienced paddler and a teacher at his middle school. This was her first year teaching, and he had heard good things about her. Word traveled fast about teachers at his school. She had graduated from the University of Georgia the previous year and looked like she could have been in high school. Kayden found her and Mr. Sullivan very easy to talk to. The topics varied. Kayden liked meeting new people and connected with Jo's dad. Mr. Sullivan and his wife had retired two years earlier and bought a sailboat. They had spent the winter island hopping in the

Bahamas. Stories of their sailing adventures helped the miles pass easily on the way to the river.

The parking lot for the Opa River put-in was large and recently paved. It was early in the season, and there were only two vehicles unloading. As he stepped out of the jeep, Kayden noticed two large signs about the dangers of the Opa River. He liked to read and walked over to the first sign for a closer look. His palms began to sweat as he read the information about dangerous rapids, emergency exits, slippery rocks, wild animals, and steep terrain. The sign also stated that paddlers had died on this river and to proceed at your own risk.

The second sign had a picture about the history of the river. The Opa River was created by water carving through sedimentary rock for thousands of years. The gorge was deep and received direct sunlight for about five hours a day. The area was known for its natural beauty and designated as a Wild and Scenic River by the federal government. This protected the river from roads and development but made access difficult.

Kayden and Mr. Sullivan helped Jo untie the boats and gather the gear from the back of the jeep. Kayden looked carefully in his duffel and retrieved the necessary items: life jacket, spray skirt, helmet, rope, bag lunch, and emergency kit. He carefully slid his paddle into his boat before hoisting it onto his shoulder. Comfort was important when carrying a kayak and gear. It had to be balanced right or it hurt your shoulders, back, and neck. The distance to the put-in was longer on the Opa River and required a half-mile hike. Kayden noticed Jo's boat and paddle were perfectly balanced on her shoulder as she started her trek toward the river.

The hike down to the river was steep, and Kayden was intrigued by the natural beauty around him. He had walked the trails to many rivers before, but today seemed different. He wasn't sure why. Kayden was excited about meeting his friends and knew they were in for a challenge. The Opa River was well known for its unforgiving nature. His early interest in rivers had become a fascination with them, and he was excited to be in the presence of water—*any* water. He enjoyed reading adventure books on the subject. *The Adventures of Huckleberry Finn* was a favorite, and Kayden had learned a lot about Tom Sawyer and the mighty Mississippi River.

The Opa River was less known but had a unique name and history. According to his whitewater guidebook, *opa* was a Greek word with two meanings. One emphasized the celebration of life; the other stressed the importance of remaining alert to danger, seeking opportunities, and being vigilant along life's path. Kayden thought it was a near-perfect name for a river.

It was the first week of May, and spring was Kayden's favorite time of year. The sky was a steely blue, and the sun warmed his body. There were small, wispy cirrus clouds moving swiftly across the sky. Days like this reminded Kayden of how much he enjoyed time on the river with his friends. Every trip was unique, and he was sure today would be no different.

Although Kayden had been kayaking for six years, he had only two years of experience on whitewater rivers. He had practiced his skills and could control his kayak in all but the most challenging rapids. He had been on eleven whitewater trips, far more than a typical twelve-year-old. Each trip was clearly etched in his mind, and he had learned an incredible amount about the challenges of paddling whitewater rivers. There were always obstacles to watch for, and the wrong decision could bring consequences, some of which he preferred not to think about. Kayden also enjoyed the calmer stretches of the rivers, and when floating along them, his mind would often drift like the eagles soaring in the distance.

Kayden had experienced a lot in his life, and he knew more changes awaited him. The river was his place of refuge. He yearned for more days like this. His life was complicated, and some of the challenges he had faced had been extremely painful and, at times, overwhelming. Because his father had recently passed away, he knew more about hardship than most kids his age.

As Kayden neared the river, he heard several familiar voices, but their words were muffled by the rush of water cascading over ledges. His feet were starting to hurt as the weight of the kayak pressed hard on his shoulder, leading Kayden to wonder if there might be water lurking in the boat from a previous trip. The weight and power of water was something to consider; even a gallon or two inside his boat could make it hard to control. Just one gallon would add more than eight pounds to his load. Kayden had learned a lot about moving water; the faster it moved, the more force it created. This explained how dead trees could be found on the tops of large boulders in the river. Kayden had a healthy respect for the powerful force of water on the river. One poor decision could lead to painful consequences. He was not the type of person to back down from a challenge, and he was also quick to learn from his mistakes.

May is one of the best months for kayaking because of the spring rains. The heavy downpours soak the mountains, forcing the water down the mountainsides to the nearest stream or river. The large volume of water, aided by gravity, flows fast over rocks and logs, creating large and powerful rapids. The river becomes more dangerous, and kayakers must be careful when paddling around large boulders or dropping over small waterfalls. The water was also very cold since it received little direct sunlight each day. Kayden hoped his wetsuit would protect him from the frigid temperature. He also wore thin, insulated gloves and carried basic safety items with him for use in the event of an emergency. Inside his bag was a cell phone, a knife, matches, and a foil blanket. He hoped he would never need them.

The trip leader was Will Sully, and Kayden liked him a lot. Will had been paddling for more than twenty-five years and had experience on some of the most challenging rivers in the country. He had a calm and reassuring manner and encouraged everyone on his trips. Will had an instinct for the river, and always seemed to choose a safe route down the rapids. His skills had been perfected over time. He often laughed about how experience had been his best teacher.

Jo was the other trip leader. She was more reserved than Will and listened more than she spoke. This skill suited her well as a new middle-school teacher. While she was a strong paddler, Jo loved the experience of just being on the water surrounded by beautiful scenery and the sounds of birds. She was an avid bird-watcher and once missed an entrance to a rapid while gazing skyward toward a bald eagle. But, she'd said, it had been worth it!

This paddling trip included two kayakers close to Kayden's age whom he had met before. Mark Meton was thirteen and had been paddling for three years. He was big for his age and well known at school. Kayden saw Mark in the hallways between classes and did not like what he saw. Mark would shove students out of his way and get close to girls, too close. Sometimes he would whisper in their ears. Kayden could not hear what he said, but the girls never smiled and instead appeared uneasy around him. He avoided

Mark if he could by talking to his friends longer or sneaking into a teacher's classroom.

Mark had a quick temper and had punched a smaller student the previous year during a game of basketball. Mark had been charging toward the basket when he had stumbled and fell. He had thought the other student had tripped him on purpose. A brief fight had broken out, and Mark had been pulled away by several teachers. Two of Kayden's friends had seen the fight and told him about it. They were glad the teachers had stopped it since Mark had looked out of control. He had cussed at the teachers as he was pulled away.

Mark was a strong paddler but lacked experience on the river. He was also quick to brag about skills he did not have. He did not listen well and did what he wanted to do. Kayden noticed this and remembered to be careful around him. Mark acted cocky, and Kayden did not trust him.

Jenny Brooks was also on the trip. Kayden had met her several times before at the lake near his home. She looked older than most thirteen-year-old girls and had been kayaking since she was six. Jenny was a natural paddler and had kayaked rivers throughout the southeastern part of the United States. She had a smooth paddling style. Her kayak seemed to almost dance across the waves and glide down the river. Jenny also had a confident Eskimo roll, a self-rescue technique first used by Eskimos to flip their kayaks upright after a capsize. Jenny could roll her boat upright in nearly any situation on the river. She had perfected this skill during countless hours in the lake near Kayden's home.

Kayden liked Jenny a lot and was always comfortable around her. She was confident but never bragged about her paddling skills. He thought she was very pretty, and he would often find any excuse to be around her. He felt a strong connection to her and recognized that she was different from other girls he knew. She had a special quality that Kayden found difficult to put into words. He found himself smiling more when he was around her.

On his last kayaking trip, Kayden had learned several new paddle strokes to help himself out of difficult situations. His paddle felt more comfortable in his hands now, and he understood that the small movements he made with it were what guided his kayak down a rock-strewn river. Kayaking required strength, but to Kayden's surprise, skill and finesse were more important. It always looked easy when he watched elite paddlers on YouTube skillfully guide their crafts over large drops in the river and around massive boulders. There were many hazards to avoid that could result in serious injury or drowning. Downed trees and undercut ledges could trap a kayaker underwater. Kayden knew this sport was not for the faint of heart.

He was proud of his newest skill, the Eskimo roll, although he had not mastered it yet. He had watched Jenny learn it and realized that it required a lot of practice. There was something very unnatural about being upside down in a boat while holding your breath underwater. He was often unsure of which way was up. After many hours of practice, he had learned to roll his kayak upright in calm water. He had not attempted to do so in fast-flowing water.

This was Kayden's first trip on the Opa River, and he was curious to see if it would live up to its tough reputation. This river was unlike any other he had paddled. The rapids were very narrow with lots of water flowing between boulders. This created powerful blasts of water and swirling currents that could easily flip a kayak. There were also waterfalls, some as high as eight feet. As part of his preparation, Kayden asked Will what to expect.

"Well, Kayden, you are in for a new experience," Will said, "and you need to be ready. The Opa River's reputation is for real. Be ready for the waterfalls and carefully choose your route down each rapid. You need to be in *the zone* on this one."

The zone. Kayden knew the term well. Will had described it on the first day of the paddling clinic Kayden had attended two years earlier. Will had written a detailed description on the whiteboard. *The Zone: a mental state of being totally connected to the present moment with no doubt or fear in your mind; an ideal connection between your mind and body that provides peak performance.*

To illustrate the concept, Will had shared several videos of top paddlers navigating extreme rapids, including fifty-foot waterfalls. Kayden had been in awe that the kayakers could navigate and survive such extreme conditions. It had made his hands sweaty just thinking about it. Will had stressed that being in the zone could help paddlers survive any challenges encountered on the river— and in life too.

Kayden refocused on the early morning mist that covered the river, casting a coolness along the riverbank. In the distance he heard the low rumble of water cascading down falls. A shiver ran through his body. His blueberry-pancake breakfast began to churn in his stomach, and he thought he might throw up. His mind began to drift. As he surveyed his surroundings, a surge of energy shot through him, his heart began to pound, and his palms began to sweat.

Kayden looked up and down the river and was struck by its natural beauty. The water was clear; he could see fish along the bottom and rocks—more than there had been in other rivers he had paddled. Large boulders were scattered about the riverbed, making it difficult to see what was coming next. Some were massive and blocked half the width of the river, forcing a lot of water into narrow spaces. Kayden marveled at several large downed trees that teetered atop some of the boulders. He wondered how such large objects could come to be perched so high up, as if they'd been dropped by a giant crane. He learned the answer to this question from his paddling guide.

A natural, free-flowing body of water, the Opa River was prone to flooding, especially during the heavy spring rains. The tree trunks were relics of high-water days. Kayden could only imagine the extreme force of the water that it took to deposit such large trees on top of the boulders. He was amazed by the power of water and knew the force of it could get him into major trouble if he made a mistake on the river. This was part of the attraction of kayaking, and Kayden knew each decision he made on the river mattered. If something went wrong, he would likely be on his own to save himself.

Will called everyone together on the sandy shore to discuss the trip and review basic safety procedures. Problems could develop quickly on the river, and accidents could happen without warning. Kayden had read several articles about paddlers who had been trapped underwater in their kayaks. One account had made him especially nervous: a kayaker had become pinned underwater when the bow of his kayak got lodged between two rocks on its way over a four-foot waterfall. The paddler had survived by leaning forward onto the front of his kayak, forming a small air pocket that allowed him to breathe.

As Will reviewed basic river safety skills, Kayden noticed Jenny was listening carefully to every word. Her eyes were focused, and she nodded each time he covered a key point. Mark, on the other hand, was clearly uninterested and staring down the river. He was a good athlete but obviously did not care to listen to others. This made Kayden uneasy around Mark, and Kayden made a mental note to be wary of him on the river. Kayden had an intuitive nature and had learned to trust his instincts. This had paid off for him on a previous adventure.

When Will finished his safety talk, Kayden walked to the edge of the river. As he stared at the sandy beach, a disturbing memory from the previous spring's paddling trip replayed in his mind in scary detail. It was supposed to have been an easy trip on the Etowah River, except for one part. The river runs through a tunnel that was used for mining in the late 1800s. The mine shaft is usually clear and safe to navigate as long as no logs or other debris are blocking it. In his mind, Kayden could still hear the voices of the two teenagers he'd been with telling him to follow them. He had not.

Having had a bad feeling about the tunnel, Kayden had made sure he was the first paddler to reach the entrance and check it out. As he had approached, he could not see any light at the end of it. This was a sure sign that it was blocked. He had immediately blown his whistle three times, alerting the other paddlers to stop. As the teens had gazed into the entrance, the danger was clear. Both had stared at Kayden for a moment and then nodded, reluctantly thanking him. Entering the mine tunnel would have resulted in serious injury or death, and they knew it. Kayden had learned something from every one of his river trips. Today's trip on the Opa River would be no different, but what he learned from it would change his life forever.

Chapter 2

"It's not what happens to you,
but how you react to it that matters."

—Epictetus

As he did at the start of every river trip, Kayden felt both excitement and worry when preparing to enter his kayak. He made sure to relieve himself within the privacy of a cluster of trees. He had learned this was an important ritual before securing his body into the boat. As he returned to the riverbank, the white mist drifted skyward. His heart beat faster when he slid into his kayak.

Whitewater kayakers need to wear a rubber spray skirt that keeps the boat watertight. Comfort is important and requires precise positioning of the body in the cockpit before sealing it with the spray skirt. If the spray skirt is not secured tightly around the lip of the cockpit, cold water enters and sloshes around in the kayak. Aside from making the paddler uncomfortably wet and cold, such a leak can cause the kayak to become very heavy and hard to steer.

Kayden tucked his long blond hair carefully into his helmet and tightly cinched his chin strap. He was ready.

Will and Jo gave the go-ahead to launch, and Kayden and the other paddlers eased gently into the river. The water at the put-in was calm, and the kayakers spent a few minutes warming up. Kayden gripped his paddle firmly as he practiced his strokes. As a trip leader, Will had established an order for the paddlers. Will took the lead spot, and Mark, Kayden, and Jenny followed, each about twenty-five feet apart. Jo took the sweep position at the end of the line. Kayden had learned that the best practice was to have the strongest paddlers at the front and rear of the line, creating a "safety sandwich." Kayden liked being in the middle so he could watch the way the lead paddler handled the oncoming rapids. He also liked knowing there was a skillful paddler behind him just in case he got into trouble.

Kayden always enjoyed the first part of any river trip. He was reconnecting with his kayak, and warming up was important for him. He shifted about in the boat, stretching his arm, back, and shoulder muscles, twisting his upper body in odd-looking positions. After completing his stretching ritual, Kayden picked up his paddle and squeezed it tightly. It was light and strong. He noticed his name and phone number written across both blades in his dad's distinctive handwriting. *Kayden Barrett, 555-0116.*

The first few minutes on the river were often uneasy for Kayden as he rediscovered the paddle strokes needed to guide his kayak. On good days, the kayak felt like an extension of his body, as if his boat were joined to his hip. He liked days when he really connected with his boat and was able to easily steer it through the rapids. This sensation of connection, being in the zone, was powerful, and Kayden longed for it. After ten minutes on the

Opa River, Kayden sensed a tight connection with boat, body, and water. He was ready yet cautious. He knew to be aware of the river's power, especially when the water plunged over rocks or ledges, which could lead to the formation of what kayakers call *hydraulics*—powerful and lethal currents that can trap paddlers underwater.

Will completed a final safety check with the paddlers to make sure everyone was ready. There was an air of excitement as he grinned at his eager group and pointed down the river. His voice was loud and clear as he nodded in Kayden's direction and said, "Let's roll!"

Kayden found a small wave on the river and slowly nudged his kayak forward. The front of his kayak moved gently back and forth as it rode along on the wave. The sensation of surfing was much to his liking, a sense of freedom and connection that just seemed right. As he surfed off the wave, he pointed his kayak down the river.

Will's voice pierced the sound of the moving water. "Eddy right!" he called.

Kayden steered his kayak toward the calm spot on the right side of the river. Eddies are calm places in the water where the currents are weak or nonexistent, and kayakers know them as welcome breaks. Kayden had learned that whitewater kayaking required eddy hopping, paddling from one calm spot on the river to the next. As his boat slipped into the calm water of the eddy, he saw that Will was there but Mark was not. Kayden was startled by a sudden thud on the back of his kayak. Mark had somehow fallen behind Kayden and slammed the front of his kayak over the back of Kayden's! The sudden impact spun Kayden's kayak to the right, and he nearly flipped over.

Will had an aggravated look on his face and yelled, "Hey, Mark! Pay attention and watch what you are doing. Stay in position!"

Mark muttered something unintelligible under his breath.

Jenny had watched Mark's careless behavior and gave him a disapproving look as she gracefully passed him, arching the bow of her kayak into the eddy. Kayden made eye contact with Mark and raised a lone eyebrow at him. Mark shook his head and back paddled several feet behind Kayden and out of his line of sight. This was not the beginning to the trip that Kayden had hoped for. He examined the front of his spray skirt to make sure it was secure and was pleased to see Jenny pull alongside him. She smiled his way, and Kayden felt butterflies in his stomach. There was something special about her smile, and he knew it was one of the many reasons she had so many friends. Kayden saw Jo speaking with Mark about his irresponsible behavior and Mark nodding in agreement. Kayden appreciated Jo defending him. He decided to be aware of Mark's location on the river at all times.

"All right, guys, it is game on!" said Will with a contagious grin on his face. "Our first challenging rapid is right around the bend, so be ready! Stay river-right and follow the standing waves. At the bottom of the rapid is a 'pillow rock,' so be extra careful."

Kayden knew that *pillow rock* was a term used to describe a rock that was barely covered with water. Such an obstacle could be tricky since any impact with a solid object could flip a kayaker upside down. As the paddlers entered the rapid, Kayden noticed that Mark was following closely behind Will as they started down the frothy waterway. Kayden heard Will's excited voice call out as they entered the rapid: "Not too close, Mark; give me some space!"

The waves were two to three feet high, so Will's and Mark's kayaks disappeared at the bottom of each one. As Kayden entered the churning water, he could not contain his excitement. A big grin spread across his face. The sensation of floating over large standing waves was thrilling and reminded him of an amusement park roller coaster! His kayak moved faster and faster as the water constricted and headed toward the pillow rock. As he approached it, he kept a good view of Mark. Paddling with all his strength, Mark went right over the top of the rock. When he landed on the other side of it, his kayak disappeared briefly into the swirling currents. Then Mark nearly flipped over! He used his paddle to brace and remain upright.

As Kayden's kayak accelerated, he realized it was moving toward the pillow rock at such an angle that his boat would hit the rock dead center. Collisions with rocks were common for kayakers, but this rock was bigger than he had thought, and the force of the water was stronger than he had realized. All he could do was get ready for the impact. His instructors had instilled in Kayden the importance of leaning into obstacles on the river when he knew he would hit them, but this went against Kayden's instinct. In a moment of hesitation, he did just the opposite of what he had been taught; he leaned upstream, away from the rock. In less than a second, Kayden was upside down in his kayak as powerful currents forced him down the river toward large underwater boulders!

Kayden's body shuddered at the impact of an underwater rock against the top of his helmet. It was a glancing blow but certainly unnerving. He had trained to rescue himself in this circumstance and was confident he would be able to roll his kayak upright in a rapid. Yet somehow this seemed different. He could not see his paddle, and the force of the water was trying to rip it from his hands. A burning developed in his chest as air was sucked out of his body through his mouth and nostrils. He felt an unbearable pressure inside, a strong and powerful force taking over, building toward panic. Kayden knew what to do; he had practiced it at least a hundred times. He leaned forward over the bow of his kayak and forced his paddle toward the surface of the water, holding it parallel to his kayak. This was known as the "set position." When his paddle was by the side of his kayak, he began his sweep stroke across the surface of the water while simultaneously flicking his hips to right his kayak. His world turned from cold and chaotic to blue sky, and best of all, he could breathe!

Kayden gulped in deep breaths. Success! He heard loud shouts from behind him. He turned to see Will paddling toward him with a big grin on his face.

"Well done, Kayden!" he said. "Your first combat roll!"

His expression said a lot, and Kayden knew that Will was proud of him. As Kayden shook his head to clear the water from his helmet, he heard a welcome voice from behind his boat. Jenny had paddled hard to catch up to him when she saw him flip.

Her worried look vanished when she saw that Kayden was okay. "So, that was some serious underwater rock study you had," she said, "but nice roll! I've seen a lot of kayakers swim on that rapid, but you made it look easy!"

Kayden smiled back at Jenny and was glad she was close by. He was pleased she thought his roll looked easy, but in reality, it had not been. The water was more violent than he'd expected, and he'd almost had his paddle snatched from his hand. Kayden remembered what Will had told him repeatedly: "Your combat roll has to be automatic. Practice until you don't even have to think about it!" Kayden had practiced his self-rescue techniques, and it had paid off. He realized that rolling his kayak in a rapid was a major accomplishment, and he could feel his confidence growing.

Will directed the group to the nearest eddy on the right side of the river by an old railroad bridge. While they rested, Kayden could not help but marvel at the water in the Opa River. It was a clear and vibrant blue. He saw Jo gazing into the river with contentment. As he drew near, she looked up and smiled directly at him.

"Well now, if it isn't Captain Cool!" she exclaimed. Jo had seen Kayden flip and was proud of his ability to stay focused and calm in a challenging situation. Given Kayden's experience with hardship, she was not surprised. "Hey, Kayden, I saw you go over on the pillow rock and lean upstream. Remember to lean downstream when you hit something, but I must say, your roll was impressive!"

Jo had a natural way of encouraging others on the river and in the classroom. There was something about the way she talked to them. Her voice and smile put people at ease. Kayden was thankful that Jo was paddling with him today. He knew he could trust her and Will to be there in the event of trouble. He was also glad that Jenny had seen him recover from his mistake, and he was relieved that he had not had to "wet exit," or swim from his kayak when he'd flipped. Paddlers often have to resort to a wet exit, especially when they are learning. Kayden did not want to be embarrassed—especially in front of Jenny—and would work hard to avoid capsizing again!

As Kayden relaxed in the calm water, he detected movement with his peripheral vision and glanced toward the middle of the river. Will was paddling his kayak gently upriver and surfing on a small wave. The bow moved gently from left to right. Even from fifty feet away, Kayden could see the pleasure on Will's face. Kayaking was like nothing else Kayden had ever experienced, and the freedom and power provided by the river was rewarding. Will surfed off the wave and headed toward Kayden, Jenny, and Jo. As he approached, he leaned into the eddy. Mark was downstream, and Will signaled for him to join them.

When Mark arrived, Will got more serious. "All right," he said, "now it is time to get really focused on the next section. Game on!" Will gathered the paddlers together and explained in detail how to enter the next rapid, which was known as Hell's Gate. "You need to move toward right-center on the river," he told them, "and head for the center of the two boulders marking the approach. You will paddle over a three-foot drop, and the river will try to push you to the right. Be sure to angle your bow slightly left and paddle hard. At all costs, avoid being swept to the right after the drop. There are undercut rocks and large boulders with swirling currents. This spot is called the Room of Doom. Make sure you stay clear!"

Kayden took Will's directives seriously and felt his heart rate increase. Mark was next to him but was staring across the river at a lone fisherman. Kayden was unsure Mark was listening. He could not help but ask, "Did you catch that, Mark? Which way do you enter the drop?"

Mark rolled his eyes. "Hey, I got this," he replied. "You just worry about yourself."

Kayden wasn't surprised at Mark's response and slowly backed his kayak away from Mark's. He decided he would keep a safe distance from him on the river. Unfortunately, Kayden knew, paddlers did not always stay in order; following too close, or too far behind, could cause big problems.

"Does anyone have questions?" Will asked to make sure that everyone knew how to run the rapid. As an added safety measure, he asked Jo to follow him down first so she could set a safety rope at the bottom of the first drop. Jo would be positioned to throw a rescue bag with fifty feet of line to any paddler who had problems and was swept toward the Room of Doom. "Plan for the best but prepare for the worst" was a mantra of safe paddling. Kayden appreciated his trip leader's safety-minded approach. As Will and Jo prepared to leave the eddy, Kayden noticed that the wispy, high clouds that had feathered the sky during their hike down to the river had given way to faster-moving gray clouds. The wind picked up, and Kayden detected a slight chill in the air. Sudden changes in weather could complicate river trips, especially if a low-lying fog developed on the water. Visibility was essential to safe river running, and Kayden knew fog could cause major complications with little to no warning.

Will and Jo left the eddy and steered their boats into a fast-moving ribbon of water. They were about fifty feet apart, and Kayden could see Will heading directly toward the middle of the two boulders. He quickly disappeared after his kayak shot over the first drop. Jo soon followed. There was an eerie calm in the eddy as Kayden, Mark, and Jenny prepared for their turns. Managing fear is an important part of paddling dangerous rivers, and all three of the remaining kayakers were feeling an odd mix of fear and excitement. Waiting was the worst part.

Mark was next in line and waited for the signal that he could enter the rapid. He saw Will standing downriver atop one of the entrance boulders holding his paddle vertically, the sign that all was clear and Mark could start his approach. Without a word, Mark left the calm waters and paddled aggressively upriver before leaning downstream with the current. Known as a "peel out," this maneuver could provide a paddler with added speed and control upon entering a rapid; it could also be dangerous because leaning even slightly upstream could cause a paddler to flip. Mark's peel out appeared to have been successful, but to his surprise his boat hit slower-moving water impeded by a big rock, and the bow swung swiftly to the left. With little warning, the strong current struck the left side of Mark's kayak, causing him to flip upstream! He was upside down in his kayak and moving directly toward the entrance boulders to Hell's Gate. Kayden saw Mark's kayak tremble up and down, and his red helmet suddenly popped to the surface. Mark had exited his boat and was being swept toward the two boulders marking the entrance to Hell's Gate.

The current was strong, and Kayden knew this was a bad situation. Mark had few options other than to try to reach a small eddy on the left side of the river. He put his head down and swam with every bit of effort he could muster to break free from the deadly grasp of the rapid that was pulling him toward the large rocks beside the Room of Doom. Mark drew close to the calm water and slowly rose to his feet. He threw his body forward toward a narrow strip of sand and landed on his stomach on the small beach. Kayden breathed a sigh of relief.

Mark stood slowly up and looked around to see who was watching. He glanced in Kayden's direction, and their eyes met but only for a second. Kayden raised his hand, palm forward, toward Mark. The message was universal and clear: stop. Mark would need to stay where he was for now. Surely Mark knew and understood Kayden's hand signal. A rescue would take time and planning.

Chapter 3

*"Your hardest times often lead to the greatest moments of your life.
Keep going. Tough situations build strong people in the end."*

—Roy T. Bennett

Mark's exit from his kayak in the rapid did not surprise Kayden or Jenny. Mark seldom practiced his self-rescue techniques yet bragged about his ability to roll his kayak. Kayden had never seen Mark roll his boat and knew he was in a dangerous situation. He felt a bump on the side of his kayak as Jenny drew in next to him. She had an expression on her face that Kayden had not seen before, and it concerned him. Jenny pulled herself next to him and leaned close so he could hear her over the roar of the water in the distance.

"Kayden, Mark is in trouble!" she said. "Go on down the rapid and make sure to angle your bow left as you approach the entrance boulders. I'll be close behind and see if we can help him. Where did his boat go?" Kayden straightened his back and scanned down the river where Mark had parted ways with his kayak. He could see him but not his kayak.

Kayden knew there could be no hesitation. He took two quick breaths, focused his mind, and paddled slightly upstream into the current. At just the right moment, he leaned downstream and began paddling vigorously toward the twin boulders marking the entrance to Hell's Gate. He was right on the entrance line paddling strongly with even strokes. As he drew near, he paddled with all his might on the right side of his boat to turn the front of his kayak slightly to the left. This was exactly where he hoped to be as the boulders loomed closer. As the kayak gained speed toward the boulder, Kayden searched everywhere for Mark. He finally saw a red object, Mark's helmet. It was perched behind a boulder high above the water. The helmet disappeared behind the boulder, and seconds later Kayden felt a powerful blow to the back of his boat. Mark's fear-stricken voice shouted, "Paddle, Kayden, straight ahead!"

As Mark's chest struck the stern of Kayden's kayak, the added weight on the rear lifted the bow, making the boat all but impossible to control. Kayden knew he had to position his bow precisely as he approached the massive boulders. With Mark clinging to the end of the kayak, Kayden leaned forward as far as he could in the hope of lowering the front and gaining more control. Kayden yelled for Mark to pull himself farther forward on the rear deck to help balance the boat. Kayden dug his paddle into the water on the right side of his kayak with all his might, trying to move his bow to the left. The twin boulders marking the entrance to Hell's Gate appeared quickly, and Kayden knew he was getting too close. His arms and shoulders burned as he used all his strength to angle his bow left. The river narrowed and the water surged as he approached the first drop on Hell's Gate. Kayden felt the kayak accelerate faster and faster. It seemed like a roller coaster ride gone horribly wrong. As he entered the drop, Kayden saw his bow lift due to Mark's deathlike grip on the rim of the cockpit. As the force of the waterfall hit the back of his boat, the stern sank. The bow was lifted straight up, like a rocket ready to launch, as a ferocious current gripped the back deck. Kayden was cast upside down into a torrent of foaming, frothing turbulence.

He attempted to set his paddle to roll the boat when an immense force ripped the paddle from his hands. As it was swept away, Kayden knew he was in a dire situation. He was being battered by powerful forces and had no way of rolling his kayak upright. He had seen more advanced paddlers roll their boats without a paddle. This was a skill he wished he had at this moment, but for now, Kayden's only option was to exit. He reached for the emergency loop on the front of his cockpit and pulled it directly toward him. As the spray skirt released, Kayden immediately put both hands on the sides of his cockpit and pushed with all his strength. His head popped up and he gasped for air. He caught a quick glimpse of Mark's helmet bobbing toward a small, sandy beach, his arms and feet in motion propelling him toward it. Kayden's view of Mark disappeared as the current pulled his body backward and then downward.

Kayden knew he was in trouble. Churning hydraulics are dangerous for kayakers. Water dropping over ledges recirculates, creating a strong circular motion that is very hazardous and sometimes impossible to escape. As he tumbled in the hydraulic, he couldn't tell which way was up. He became disoriented and felt his lungs begin to burn as his need for oxygen increased. He felt himself start to weaken, and he could tell he had little strength left to combat the force of the water. As his body went limp, he was pulled deeper and deeper. The flow of the currents shifted in a different direction at the bottom, providing an out-ward flow of water that Kayden could use to escape. He abruptly shot to the surface, desperately gasping for air.

Although disoriented, he heard a loud voice that seemed close. Jo was perfectly positioned along the shore, safety rope in hand as he surfaced less than forty feet away. He was glad to hear her voice.

"Rope!" she called. "Catch the rope, Kayden!"

He felt a nylon rope hit his hands and attempted to clasp his fingers around it. He had to hang on! Kayden felt the tension become tighter and realized he was being pulled down the river. The strength of rushing water was incredible. He had been trained to roll over on his back when using a rescue rope. This allowed him to keep his head above water and breathe.

Kayden glanced to his left and saw the steep boulders along the river. They were larger than he had expected, and the water was moving with tremendous power. He knew he had to hold tightly to the rope or risk being swept into the Room of Doom. His heart was racing as he held on with every ounce of his energy. His lungs burned, and his arms were weakened by his time underwater. He could no longer hold on. The rope was violently ripped from his hands. Kayden sensed the immense force of the water on his body; it was like a jet stream from a fire hose, and it was moving him toward the base of a large boulder where the water seemed to disappear.

The Opa River was known for its undercut rocks, and there were rumors of underwater caverns and caves. This was precisely where Kayden did not want to be. He attempted to swim out of the powerful current as the large boulders grew closer. He was out of options and could only pray and hope the flow of the water would sweep him around, and not under, the boulder. He shifted his body around to fend off the boulder with his feet. This action, much to his horror, did not help as the strong currents shoved him underneath the giant rock marking the entrance to the Room of Doom. His world became pitch black. The turbulence of the water pummeled his body into rock walls. He realized that he was in the worst possible situation. It had happened so quickly.

Kayden's mind raced with fear as he was plunged farther into the depths of the river. Would this be the end? How would he survive? As his lungs were about to explode, he felt his body suddenly shoot to the surface. Engulfed by darkness, Kayden gulped in large amounts of air and coughed up water from his lungs. He had nearly drowned, and his senses were overwhelmed. As he forced his mind to focus, he had a startling and frightening realization. He was trapped in an underwater cavern, enveloped in complete darkness. Kayden felt around for something to grab, anything at all, but could only feel frigid water rushing past him! The sound of quickly moving water is unique. The faster it moves, the louder it becomes, ultimately creating a deafening roar.

Kayden sensed he was moving but had no way of knowing which way to swim to get to safety. He was aware of the loud roar drawing closer by the second. With little to no control over his situation, he swung his feet toward the direction of the loud sound and crossed his hands over this chest. He knew shifting his body would provide some degree of protection and might cushion his impact with rocks or boulders. The sound of the crashing water filled his ears. His mind filled with dread. Without warning, Kayden felt his legs drop out from underneath him, and then he was falling, tumbling through space, and gaining speed at an alarming rate. For the first time in his life, Kayden felt totally helpless. He was terrified and completely on his own.

Chapter 4

"You should never give up. No matter how hard the situation is, always believe that something beautiful is going to happen."

—Gudapati Srikanth

Jo was standing near the spot where Kayden disappeared. She simply could not believe her eyes: did that just happen? She had been at the best spot on the river to rescue Kayden when she saw his problems begin. It had happened right in front of her! Despite the odds, all the possible negative outcomes had occurred at the same time. Murphy's Law was evident on the river: anything that could go wrong would go wrong. As these thoughts raced through her mind, Jo realized she had to act quickly if she had any chance of saving Kayden's life. Kayakers who are trapped underwater have, at the most, two to three minutes before they drown. If the river is cold, survival may be extended since frigid water slows the heart rate and temporarily reduces the brain's need for oxygen.

Jo forced all of the air in her lungs into her whistle three times. Will immediately turned his head from the eddy fifty feet downriver. He had expected his group to arrive any moment and was growing anxious. Delays are not uncommon on the river, but Will sensed there might be something wrong upriver. Jo's three short bursts on her whistle were loud, and Will knew right away that there was an emergency. Even from his position downstream, he could see the fear on Jo's face. She was signaling with rapid circular arm movements, indicating she urgently needed help.

Will wasted no time. He paddled upstream with a fierce determination and directed his kayak toward Jo. The water was moving against him, but the current was weak along the eddy line. Propelling a kayak against the flow of moving water is known as "ferrying," and Will was a master at it. He closed in on Jo's position on the rock. She was pacing anxiously back and forth, grasping the rescue bag with fifty feet of uncoiled rope dangling from her hands.

"Hurry, Will, hurry!" she shouted. "Kayden disappeared under a rock, and I can't spot him!"

Will knew all too well that this was a worst-case scenario for any kayaker. Undercut rocks often trap a variety of debris such as logs, limbs, and even tree trunks. These types of obstructions form lethal sieves, capable of entrapping kayakers in an underwater tomb. Paddling even harder, he leaned back so the bow of his kayak would slide onto a rock. He yanked the loop on his skirt and leaped from his boat, all in one deft motion. He covered the short distance to Jo, his eyes scanning the riverbed for any signs of Kayden. As his heart and mind raced, he glanced back at Jo. Her expression of shock and horror had been replaced by one of sheer determination to locate Kayden.

"Follow me," Jo commanded with seriousness that Will had never heard before from her.

As they scrambled up the rocks toward the entrance to Hell's Gate, Will heard a distant rumble, followed by a loud crack of lightning! The wind picked up, and he saw dark thunderheads hovering in the distance. Will's mind was spinning with possible rescue plans. He knew that deteriorating weather would make this rescue even more treacherous, if not impossible, to execute.

"Over there, Will!" Jo yelled as she pointed toward the large boulders on the right side of the drop marking the entrance to the Room of Doom. "Kayden went directly under the large boulder on the right! I hit him with the rescue rope about fifty feet from the rock, but he could not hang on!"

Jo's gaze followed Will as he darted across the tops of the rocks in the direction of the Room of Doom. She was relieved to see Jenny and Mark standing on a small beach between two boulders. Both he and Jenny were standing by their kayaks, and Mark's head was down. Jenny was face-to-face with Mark; her cheeks were bright red and her lips were moving. Jo could not hear her words but knew she was upset with Mark. Jenny was tearing into him. Mark looked down at the sand, refusing to make eye contact with her. She was irate that Mark had panicked when Kayden had paddled past him. Jo had listened to Will's pre-trip safety review many times. He always mentioned what *not* to do if you were stranded in the middle of a rapid. Leaping onto another kayaker's boat without warning was one of many disastrous options that could make a bad situation worse. Mark's impulsive decision had put him and Kayden in grave danger, and he knew it.

Jo was glad Will was with her. She knew they had to act if there would be any chance of rescuing Kayden before he drowned. They had experienced many scary events on the river before but none with the deadly possibility of Kayden's disappearance. Jo had heard many of Will's river stories. One of the most memorable was a Chattooga River trip more than twenty years earlier. A kayaker had exited her kayak on the Five Falls section of the river and was swept under Hydroelectric Rock. This notorious rapid featured a large boulder with a narrow strainer at the front, large enough for a small paddler to fit through unless the tunnel was blocked by river debris. The paddler had disappeared through the narrow sieve for more than thirty seconds. She was extremely fortunate to be able to remove herself by placing her fingers in small crevices above her head and pulling herself through the narrow tunnel. A larger paddler would not have survived.

Jo stared at Will as he searched for Kayden. She knew his mind was racing with everything he had learned about rescuing paddlers in grim situations. With limited time at their disposal, both knew they would need to locate Kayden by studying the flow of the river. Moving water is dynamic, constantly changing depending on the conditions. Jo examined the area around the boulder where Kayden had disappeared. A large amount of water was rushing under the rock, and there was no obvious outflow. This was another very bad sign; the water was either recirculating beneath the boulder or was being drawn into a series of underwater caves. Jo saw Will's expression change and believed he was formulating a plan.

His eyebrows narrowed as he spoke. "I have a plan, Jo," he said. "It is risky, but we have no other choice. We must find Kayden from the boulders that are above or downriver from the entrance to the Room of Doom. He has to be somewhere under the boulders. We will need Jenny and Mark to help too."

Jo motioned toward Jenny and Mark with her arm, signaling them to come quickly.

Time often appears to stand still in crisis situations. As the group assembled at Will's kayak, Jo observed the faces of the others. Mark's tears had dried on his cheeks. Jenny's pupils were large, and her cheeks were red from exertion. Will's expression was more focused than she had ever seen. Everyone understood this was a deadly situation. The roar of the river was loud, and the sky had turned an even darker shade of gray. Jo listened carefully as Will spoke. His breathing was labored, but his voice remained steady.

"All right, here's what needs to happen," Will began. "Do *exactly* what I tell you to do. Jo and I are going to try to reach Kayden from the back side of the boulders that form the Room of Doom. Jenny and Mark, I need you to get your cell phones and hike back up the trail toward our start point. Cell signals are weak to nonexistent on this river. Hike up to a ridge if you need to. When you find a signal, call 911 and let them know a paddler is missing. The trail is just downriver from the Room of Doom. Go now, and remember, the trail back to our starting point is steep and treacherous. Be alert—and hurry!"

Jenny and Mark ran to retrieve their phones and began their trek toward the ridge.

Jo looked at Will. Both knew exactly what was at stake. Will grabbed his paddle and throw rope and nodded for Jo to follow. They moved over rocks and boulders to a small sandy patch just downriver from the massive boulders that formed the Room of Doom. Although their sense of time was distorted, Will guessed about two minutes had elapsed since Kayden had disappeared under the rock. The math was simple. If Kayden was underwater, they had about sixty seconds, maybe slightly more to find him before he drowned. Will listened carefully to Jo for directions to the spot Kayden had disappeared.

"This way, Will," Jo said, moving as quickly as possible toward the downriver side of the massive boulders. She knew the exact spot on the boulder where Kayden had disappeared, and moved to the location most directly downriver from there. "Will, I think this spot is in line with where Kayden should have emerged," she said.

This was a critical juncture in their rescue plan, and they both knew that Kayden's life depended on them making the right decisions. There were two options. One would be to reach Kayden by water, which meant battling against the current flowing out from the enormous boulders. The current appeared light in a few spots but surged strongly where the rocks were more constricted. The other option was to reach Kayden from above. Jo studied Will's face as they considered the choices: land- or water-based rescue? Or would it be possible to try both? Jo was reassured by the stern, determined look on Will's face. She listened carefully as he announced his plan.

"Jo, you take your rope and try to find Kayden from above," he said. "There are several access points where you might be able to see him. He could be anywhere among the boulders. I'm going to try to reach him from downstream and search the rocks with my hands and paddle. Whistle three times if you find him. Got it?"

Jo sprinted toward the boulder garden and moved swiftly from rock to rock. She quickly discovered the first access point and peered down into the spaces between the rocks. She was ten feet above the swirling waters and could see several small logs moving in circles. The waters entered the cavern from underneath two large boulders and created a strong whirlpool. The shape reminded Jo of the water exiting her bathtub when she was a child but with a ferocity she had never seen. She realized there was no sign of

Kayden in this area; even if there was, getting him out from this point was very unlikely.

Jo bolted to the next access point among the boulders; she approached the bluff very carefully. One slip and she could be trapped in a watery abyss. This access was atop the largest rocks and provided a view of the river that was daunting. As Jo peered downward, she observed a violent display of water entering the chasm from two large undercut rocks. The water surged and receded, creating a haunting gurgling sound that sent a chill down her spine. There were objects swirling in the water, most notably a five-foot-long log, an object approximately the size of Kayden. The log would spin and disappear for five and ten seconds at a time, then suddenly rocket to the surface. Jo's heart began to sink as she saw no sign of Kayden and realized that his chances for survival were growing slimmer by the second. She understood that, if he were to survive, it would be up to Will to reach him from downstream. Jo was disappointed. She could only hope and pray that Will's end of the rescue plan yielded better results. She was unable to locate Kayden, much less rescue him from the Room of Doom.

Jo maintained hope that Will would find Kayden. She had seen Will demonstrate several amazing rescues on previous river trips. He had once saved a kayaker in trouble on a monstrous rapid on the Gauley River known as Lost Paddle. The boater had flipped and was swimming for his life to avoid undercut rocks. Will paddled the victim to safety by asking him to climb on the back of his kayak. Unlike Kayden, Will had not been in a constricted entrance to a rapid at the time.

As Jo watched Will ascend the boulder garden, she could sense the urgency in his movements. Will's mind was intensely focused, almost trancelike as he initiated his rescue plan. His heart raced and his body surged with adrenaline. Jo had a clear view of him as he surveyed the waters exiting the rocks downstream from the Room of Doom. He identified the largest outflow from the boulders there. The flow of water follows the path of least resistance, and Will knew that Kayden was somewhere directly upriver from that point. But where?

Will moved along the sides of the rocks lining the shore to a point he wished to search. The depth of the water varied, and at times he stumbled in the icy cold river but managed to remain on his feet. As he neared the boulder with the most water flowing from its base, he saw small indentations in the rock, large enough for him to wedge his feet into for traction. His feet ached as he shifted his body along the base of the boulder that might give him access to where Kayden was likely trapped. When Will reached his destination, he surveyed the waterline as it rose and ebbed on the rocks. He fell to his knees and reached up under the rocks with his hands and arms to feel for any sign of Kayden. In several spots, Will used his paddle to probe the gaps. His heart pounded as he searched the area where he hoped to gain a glimpse of Kayden. Will had to find him in the next sixty seconds, or Kayden would most likely die.

As Will moved closer to the largest rock, the force of the water grew stronger and his feet grew numb. When he reached the largest boulder, he saw a crack in the left side. He located a small foothold and peered into the crevice. As Will pushed himself higher on the footing, he saw a yellow object on the surface of the water. His heart skipped as he pushed his head farther down into the gap. Water was pulsing over and under the object, which appeared to have arms that were moving up and down frantically. Kayden's life jacket was yellow! Will's body quivered as he stretched higher up the rock face for a better view.

"Kayden, Kayden! I'm here! Are you okay?" Will shouted. Will thrust his head into the gap to get a better view of the yellow object. Suddenly, his heart sank with a bleak reality. The yellow object with flailing arms was not a life jacket or Kayden. As he peered closer, he saw that it was a yellow tube approximately four feet long. It was a foam swim noodle. The tube gyrated in wild formations as the forces of the Opa River struck it from all sides. Will felt an overwhelming surge of sadness. He feared that Kayden's time had run out and dreaded that his mission would now shift from rescue to recovery. A wave of nausea washed over Will. Exhausted, he stumbled to a sandy spot near the main boulder and collapsed. His body shuddered and heaved as he vomited on the sandy shore. Kayden was gone.

Chapter 5

"The river moves, but it follows a path. When it tires of one journey, it rubs through some rock to forge a new way. Hard work, but that's nature."

—Kekla Magoon

Jenny and Mark moved carefully up the path that paralleled the Opa River. The trail was slick, and the rain and wind made the conditions treacherous. She knew the nearest parking area was at least three miles away and much of the trek would be uphill. Their water shoes were ideal for walking along the riverbanks, but the soles became clogged with mud as they attempted to hike up the slippery path. Their breathing was heavy as they moved as quickly as the conditions would permit. Jenny and Mark had placed their cell phones in clear waterproof bags to protect them from the elements. Jenny realized the importance of their mission—finding a cell signal to call 911—was their top priority. A local swift-water rescue team would be dispatched to help find Kayden, hopefully alive.

Jenny glanced behind her to check on Mark and was surprised to see him falling behind. Her gaze homed in on his face, which appeared red and swollen. It was flushed from the exertion, and he was sobbing quietly as he attempted to keep Jenny in sight. The circumstances were grim, and he knew it. Mark had acted with complete disregard for Kayden's safety and was largely responsible for the accident. Jenny recognized the expression on his face. Pain, guilt, and dread were hard to hide. The incident had occurred so unexpectedly. Was this really happening?

The trail was slippery, and small rocks crunched under their shoes as they continued up the path. Jenny recalled a recent memory of Mark sharing his book report in their English class. It was obvious that he was intelligent. Jenny realized that he was also smart enough to know the chances of finding Kayden alive were unlikely. The color in Mark's face had changed from red to gray. He looked like he might throw up. Jenny was a well-conditioned athlete and moved up the trail gracefully. Mark was strong and powerfully built but seldom exercised. He spent countless hours playing video games alone in his room. He liked the idea of working out but struggled to sustain his interest in fitness or in anything else, for that matter.

Jenny had encountered Mark on several occasions and, like Kayden, had been wary of him. She had a keen sense about people and had witnessed Mark's rude behavior toward other students. She was aware of some of Mark's past, and this softened her view of him. His life had been difficult and full of changes. His father had been arrested for dealing drugs and was recently released from prison. His parents had divorced, and he and his mom had moved twice in the past three years. Jenny had been surprised to learn that Mark had been sick the previous year and spent a week in the hospital with pneumonia. There were rumors that he had also been treated for depression in a local hospital.

Jenny was struggling to control her anger. She was more upset with Mark than she had ever been with anyone in her life. Mark had done precisely what he had been told not to do and was largely responsible for Kayden's disappearance. As intense as it was, Jenny's fury was constrained by a mysterious force within her, a core quality that her parents had instilled in her at a young age: the importance of forgiveness. Rage and hostility were capable of consuming anyone, and forgiveness was the only real antidote, especially in extreme circumstances.

The ache in Jenny's heart and the strength of her yearning for Kayden's return revealed something that she had not realized. She had many guy friends and had known that there was something different about Kayden, but only now did she allow herself to acknowledge that her feelings for him were different, far different. Her mom often spoke of *matters of the heart*, a term she used to describe relationships. It was a complicated subject. Jenny realized that she cared deeply for Kayden on many levels. He was unlike all the other boys she knew. He made her feel different. But Jenny had known to be careful. She had watched as many of her friends had gotten hurt in relationships, and she had seen how intense their pain had been.

Jenny listened to adults in her life, and many echoed a similar message: *Be careful; life can be painful at your age.* She heard it all the time and was sometimes annoyed by the frequency of the message. She liked being outside in nature, and most of her friends were boys. She liked hanging out with them. She had liked a boy named Jake when she was in sixth grade but had kept it to herself.

Her feelings for Kayden were unchartered waters for her. More than anything, she wanted to see him again.

Jenny continued her rapid pace up the trail as Mark struggled to keep up. His muffled sobbing and wheezing was painful to hear. She could tell that he was trying his best to hurry, which softened her spirit toward him. The sounds coming from him were primal. He was sad and hurting more than anyone she had ever seen. As the trail reached a divide, she paused to let him catch his breath.

The trail split in two directions. One headed back down along the riverbank, and the other continued up the side of the mountain. There were no signs for direction, and Jenny pondered which trail was best.

"Let's take the uphill trail," she told Mark after a moment of reflection. "Cell signals are more likely to be found at the top of the mountain."

Mark nodded in agreement. To her surprise, Mark proceeded past her, continuing up the trail without saying a word. His pace was now much faster. His sobbing was still audible, but less obvious than before. She detected a strong determination in his gait.

Jenny followed, keeping a careful eye on Mark as he proceeded up the trail about fifty feet ahead of her. This section of the Opa River was remote and rarely accessed. According to the sign at the put-in of the river, a variety of wildlife populated the area, most notably wild boar, coyotes, deer, rattlesnakes, copperheads, and black bears. The signs also provided recommendations for what to do when encountering wildlife. Jenny had carefully read the signs and stored this information in the back of her mind.

As Mark approached a sharp left turn in the trail, he slowed, and Jenny quickly closed the distance between them. He raised his hand above his head and slowly closed it into a fist. The unexpected signal surprised Jenny, but she understood his request to stop and remain silent. Mark stood eerily still and turned his head to the left. A simple grunt sounded in the near distance, no more than fifty feet away. Mark and Jenny shifted their gaze and scanned the woods, fearful of what they might see. Forty feet up the side of the mountain, some rhododendron bushes began to move, slowly at first. All of Mark's and Jenny's senses heightened, and the sounds, sights, and smells of the forest seemed to intensify. Another sound emerged, off to the right side of the trail. The sounds were similar but oddly muted. Mark and Jenny both shifted their gaze from one side of the trail to the other. Jenny detected movement to the left, and a large black bear emerged from the rhododendron thicket, snorting and moving in their direction. The sounds from the right side of the trail became more audible, and Mark and Jenny noticed multiple movements down the side of the mountain. Three small cubs were walking in their direction, moving slowly and deliberately up the side of the mountain, their lumbering movements constrained by gravity.

Jenny stood motionless as she pondered her options. Mark was also stationary and appeared frozen with fear.

"Mark, we are in between a mother bear and her cubs," Jenny whispered. "Don't move."

Unbeknownst to Jenny, Mark had also read the signs about wildlife and, more importantly, what to do if you encounter a black bear. Such encounters are dangerous, and more so if a hiker comes between a mother bear and her cubs. Mark paused for a moment and turned toward Jenny. His breathing slowed, and he looked her in the eye.

"Listen carefully, Jenny," he said. "Do not show fear, stand tall, and very slowly walk back down the trail. If the mother bear comes toward us, I will distract her. Go as quickly as you can to the top of the ridge and call for help!"

Jenny was encouraged that Mark was focused and had a plan. His idea was spot-on and consistent with the signs posted at the parking area. Jenny was amazed Mark knew what to do. She hoped it would work.

What happened next would be forever etched in Jenny's memory. The mother bear snorted once, looked up the side of the mountain, and started her charge. She covered the fifty feet in a matter of seconds, a guttural roar coming from deep within her. Jenny stood transfixed, and Mark stood his ground, straightening his posture as the bear drew closer. Black bears are often shy around people, but not this time, especially with this bear's cubs on the other side of the trail. As the bear closed in, Jenny began to move slowly backward just as Mark had directed. She was ten feet behind him when the bear struck Mark at full speed, slamming him to the ground with brutal force. The angry snorts and wails of the mama bear were loud, piercing the woods and reverberating off the nearby granite cliffs. Jenny could hear Mark's groans and shrieks as the bear tore at him in his huddled, protective position, hands behind his neck. She wanted desperately to help him but knew this was her only chance to escape and reach the top of the ridge to call for help. She continued to walk backward down the trail, incredulous at the sight unfolding before her eyes. Her last memory was of the mother bear standing on her hind feet and throwing her full weight on Mark as he huddled in that protective ball trying to shield himself.

Jenny pivoted 180 degrees from her brisk backward walk to a forward sprint. She had to escape this deadly encounter and raced one hundred yards down the trail to a previous spot where Mark and Jenny had rested. Her need to reach the top of the ridge was more critical than ever. Mark had been seriously wounded, if he survived the attack at all. It had been hours since Kayden had disappeared, and he had likely drowned.

As Jenny peered up the side of the mountain, she could see the summit. It was one hundred yards away, possibly more. The terrain was very steep. As Jenny scanned the ridge top, she selected a route to the top, carefully remembering natural features, including a large black boulder and two fallen trees. These would be navigation markers as she maneuvered around the thick rhododendron plants common in the Appalachian Mountains. She darted up the first twenty-five yards, her agility and fitness yielding excellent progress. The remaining seventy-five yards were slow and tedious as she clung to large roots and sought footholds on the muddy surface. She crawled on her belly under large thickets as she neared the top. Finally, the terrain leveled out, and she rose to her feet and sprinted the final ten yards to the summit. Exhausted, she reached into her plastic bag and retrieved her cell phone. Her lungs burned and both hands shook as she pressed the *on* button. She desperately needed for there to be a cell signal. More than anything, she needed help now if Kayden and Mark were to have any chance of surviving. As her phone came to life, she scanned the top of her screen. Tears began to stream down her face as she looked at the signal strength bars. Not one but two bars appeared. She took two deep breaths as her fingers danced over the keypad: 9-1-1.

"Hello, this is Jenny," she said when the operator answered, "and I need to report an emergency."

Chapter 6

"Hope is seeing light in spite of being surrounded by darkness."

—Desmond Tutu

Kayden's body gathered speed as he plummeted over the waterfall in the dark cavern. He was disoriented and confused as his body plunged downward. The rounded rock that stopped his fall struck his chest with a force unlike any he had experienced before. The impact knocked the air out of his lungs, leaving him gasping. The thick mist surrounding him made breathing even more difficult.

The human body gains considerable speed during a vertical drop of twelve feet. Kayden was thankful that his life jacket and helmet had absorbed some of the impact. Without them, he realized his chest and ribs would have been crushed. Even with the benefit of his safety gear, the impact caused excruciating pain to shoot throughout his body. He feared he would black out as his body went limp. His arms and legs felt numb, as if they were no longer connected to his body. Kayden had now been pummeled by the Opa River: smashed into rocks, held underwater, and thrust down a twelve-foot waterfall onto a boulder. Just how much more could he endure? His mind began to drift, and his vision began to blur. He knew he needed help to survive. ✓

The roar of the waterfall in the underwater cavern was deafening as Kayden struggled to his feet. He realized he needed to move away from the sound. He had to find refuge, but it was so dark that he didn't know where it might be. As he moved away from the roar of the waterfall, his feet slipped, and the fast-moving water took control. He instinctively positioned his feet in front of him to fend off impact with rocks. He was unsure of the depth of the water as his body bounced off rocks in the cavern. After a scary ride in the darkness, Kayden struggled to regain his footing. The current had subsided, and he groped with his hands and feet to survey his surroundings. Kayden's feet touched a sandy, firm bottom, and his spirits lifted when he stood. The water stopped just below his chest. He shuffled slowly away from the ominous sound of the waterfall and counted ten steps before he struck a wall. He stretched his hands over his head and felt nothing above. As he raised up on tiptoe, his fingers contacted solid rock directly above. Relieved, he began taking deep breaths and contemplating his circumstances. He shivered in the cold and struggled to clear his mind.

Kayden had experienced hardship before, but he had never experienced anything like this. As his breathing improved, more oxygen reached his brain and his mind began to clear. After dropping him over the waterfall, the current had forced Kayden into this small cave. His body had been battered and he was in shock. This sort of accident happened to other people, not him. He had to focus on his current problem, not the tragedy from his past. Few twelve-year-old boys had endured the trauma that Kayden had experienced. The memory haunted him every day of his life. He missed his dad now more than ever.

Kayden realized that he was on his own and needed to respond very carefully. The key was to refocus his mind and move forward. He had to take careful action in order to stay alive. His mind drifted back to a camping trip he took as a Boy Scout. One word was ingrained in his brain from that trip: preparedness. No matter where you go in life, or what you do, be prepared.

· Kayden took three more deep breaths and forced himself to concentrate on a plan to get out of the cave. As he exhaled the third time, Kayden's thoughts came into sharper focus. His heart rate slowed, and his mind began to clear. An idea started to form, hazy at first, then clearer as he began to create a plan, one step at a time. First, where was he?

As he surveyed his surroundings, Kayden stood in awe of the total darkness that engulfed him. He held his hand out directly in front of his face and could not see anything. He could hear the roar of the water as it dropped over the waterfall. The ground trembled from the impact. He was unsure about the dimensions of the cavern but estimated the ceiling height where he stood at about six feet. He was able to touch the ceiling when standing on his toes. The depth of the water was about four feet as it ebbed and flowed around his chest.

Preparedness. What did he have with him? Kayden recalled the basic survival tools needed in an emergency that had been taught him in his whitewater paddling clinic. Warmth was vital, and Kayden's feet were growing numb from the cold water. He shivered as he considered his options, searching for the next step of his escape plan. He smiled in relief as he reached for the pockets of his life jacket. Will made sure everyone in his group had basic survival items in the event of an emergency. Now Kayden understood why.

He reached his hand into the left mesh pocket of his life jacket and grasped the rectangular metal case—his cell phone! Help was a call away. As Kayden felt for the top of the plastic bag, his fingers ran along the sealing ridges used to keep water out. But the seals were apart, and water poured from the bag. The bag had been torn open, most likely from the violent forces when Kayden careened onto the boulder at the bottom of the waterfall. His hand trembled from the cold as he reached for the power button and pressed it down, hoping and praying for a light that would indicate his phone was still working. As he held the phone, his fingers pushed harder and harder on the button. His phone remained dark, and Kayden could not hide his disappointment and frustration. Kayden stretched his hand outward in the darkness and then stuffed the phone back in his life jacket. His phone was useless and would not provide the lifesaving link he so desperately needed.

Kayden leaned his head forward, trying to pierce the darkness. What else did he have with him? He reached inside the right-side pocket of his life jacket and found a cylindrical plastic container along with a small folding knife, a survival knife. His mind immediately returned to the pre-trip safety discussion that Will had provided: "All right, listen up! You should always have two items with you on the river. Make sure you have a knife in the event you are trapped in your boat and need to cut your way out. Also, keep waterproof matches in your life jackets. Next to drowning, hypothermia is one of the greatest dangers on the river. You need a way to stay warm."

Matches! Kayden knew the case was strong and tightly sealed. He shuffled his feet toward the shallow part of the cavern and reached his hands out for the wall. He was careful not to drop the matches in the darkness. He shook the water from his hands and slowly loosened the cap. After carefully removing one match, he felt the side of the case for the striking area. He gently struck the tip of the match against the surface. He smelled sulfur as the match lit and cast an eerie glow all around him. He knew this would provide at least fifteen seconds of light, so he focused and scanned his surroundings. The cavern was small with slick gray and black walls with droplets of water slowly sliding down them. The water had remained at chest level as Kayden had moved about. The fire consumed the match, and he dropped the burnt sliver into the water. He heard the match sizzle as the light faded and darkness returned.

The light cast by the match was illuminating and frightening at the same time. The water had pushed Kayden deeper into the cave, into an area larger than he thought possible. Kayden estimated the cave to be fifteen feet long and eighteen feet wide. The ceiling was shaped like a bell with the highest point about two feet over his head. As he pondered his options, a terrifying thought emerged—*the weather!*—and he battled a sense of dread. At the start of the trip, he had noticed storm clouds in the distance, and he knew any increase in the water level could seriously hinder his chances for survival. The Opa River was sensitive to rainfall and had a large watershed. This meant the water level in the river could rise and fall rapidly, depending on the weather. He had enough room to breathe for now but knew that could change very quickly. He maneuvered his body closer to the sidewall, searching for an indentation in the rock where he could sit and gather his thoughts. He shuddered from the cold and more so at the thought of the water rising slowly around him. He knew that could ultimately lead to a slow and painful death by drowning as water slowly displaced the air in the cavern. He pushed this thought from his mind.

Kayden had precious few resources but was determined to use them to the best of his ability. He had a knife, matches, and a life jacket. He was wet and cold, and his body was experiencing the early stages of hypothermia. He was beginning to shake uncontrollably. His focus was slipping, and he struggled to stay alert. He had seen wood in the cavern when the match was lit, but the logs were wet. Plus, lighting a fire would burn oxygen, a precious resource he could not afford to lose.

He knew the water was entering the cavern from the waterfall he had careened over and that the water had to be exiting the cave. But where? He had to locate the exit point. He needed light to follow the flow in the cavern, and he had more matches. Moving water was governed by the rules of physics and was, therefore, predictable. If the water could exit the cavern, perhaps he could as well.

To begin his search, Kayden wanted to examine every crevice in the cavern. He realized it would be easier to maneuver in his cramped confines if he removed his bulky life jacket. As he reached for the zipper, his hand brushed against a small metal object. His heart skipped as his fingers and brain made the connection: another tool, so simple and so needed! The small metal whistle attached to the zipper of his life jacket was only to be used in an emergency, like this one. Kayden held the whistle tightly in one hand and his plastic case of matches in the other. He now had three tools at his disposal. He continued to slide along the wall of the cavern and found a small rock outcropping to sit on.

Matches, a knife, and a whistle. Kayden had never realized that three simple items could bring such excitement—and hope! He decided to explore his surroundings further by striking another match. In a survival situation, assessment of resources was important, and he had to maximize everything at his disposal, including the matches. He gently unscrewed the cap and counted them. This was a delicate process in the dark, and Kayden was careful not to drop any in the water. He was pleased to discover thirteen matches, each good for about fifteen seconds of light. There were also two extra flints in a plastic bag that could be used. Doing the math, Kayden figured his matches would allow for a total of 195 seconds of light, or a little over three minutes; every second was valuable to devise his escape plan.

He struck a match and scanned the cave. The walls were thick and mostly smooth. Kayden had learned about rocks in school and in scouting. He believed the cavern was made of sedimentary rocks that had settled over millions of years. The rocky chamber was likely created when large plates were forced upward by powerful forces within the earth's core.

As the light from the match dimmed, he watched the direction of the current. It flowed in a circle and appeared to exit in the middle of the cavern. The image was familiar to him, like something he had seen before, but here, it was on a much larger and more powerful scale. Kayden recalled a small fleet of boats he had kept by his bathtub during his younger years. He had played with the boats and watched them spin in circles as the water drained from the tub.

Kayden's body felt weird, and his senses heightened in the dark cave. He had learned about the body's *fight-or-flight response* in health class. There was some sort of chemical released by your brain in an emergency. The word *adrenaline* came to mind, but he wasn't sure if that was right. He could feel his heart beating faster. As he inhaled, the smell was odd, a mix of fresh mountain water and decaying wood. The moving water slapped at large rocks, creating a spray that hung in the air. The force of swirling water tugged at Kayden, trying to pull him away from the safety of the rock walls. It pulled strongly at his waist, drawing him toward the center of the vortex. The water produced an eerie popping sound as it spiraled down into the vortex. He quickly retreated to the safety of the wall several feet away. As he caught his breath, Kayden realized he could have been trapped by the vortex. He had learned the term in science class in sixth grade. He distinctly remembered the examples provided: a tornado and a whirlpool. It had been a close call; Kayden knew he had to be more careful.

The whistle. Will had made sure everyone in his group had one. Kayden knew that sound carried easily over water but not through rock. It was hard to estimate their thickness, but the boulders that encased him were huge. Kayden's survival instincts told him to try the whistle since he had nothing to lose and everything to gain. With that in mind, he pulled the whistle to his lips and blew with everything he could muster. He forgot to cover his ears, and the piercing sound hurt. The next time, he covered his ears and gave the whistle another hard blow. When he stopped, Kayden could hear the shrill signal bounce against the rock walls. As the echo faded, the sound of rushing water filled his ears. He yearned for other sounds, especially human voices. Kayden had not heard another human voice for hours.

Time had begun to blur the moment Mark had leaped onto the back of Kayden's kayak. He had lost track of time but knew that the trip had begun in the late morning. They had paddled for about two hours before his accident had occurred, so it had to be around noon, twelve thirty at the latest. He was exhausted from the events on the river, and the darkness made it seem later than it was. He was unsure exactly how long he had been in the cavern. Kayden was fatigued, and his ribs hurt from the impact on the rock at the base of the waterfall. His thin wetsuit was helpful but slowly losing its effectiveness at keeping him warm.

Still, Kayden was determined to find a way out. He *had* to find a way out. He continued to assess his surroundings, shuffling slowly along with his hands on the wall and his feet surveying the bottom. As he checked his dark world, he felt a small indentation in the rock wall, maybe a foot deep and just large enough for him to sit on. He fell to his knees and shifted his butt into the odd shape in the rock wall. The bottom of the riverbed sloped upward toward the indentation, and he realized that he could sit and lean his back against the rock. The top half of his body was dry, leaving only the lower part of his legs in the water. Finally, a place of rest, at least for the moment. He took a deep breath and reached for his whistle and matches. Both items provided comfort and hope.

Kayden shifted his mind to the outside world, to what was likely happening above him. He knew that Jenny and Jo had seen him disappear down the entrance chute to the Room of Doom. From their vantage points, both most likely had seen him get swept down the chute and disappear under the rock. Jo had made a great throw with her rescue rope. If only he had been able to hold on! The water flow was incredibly strong, and the line had literally been torn from his hands. He never had a chance.

The scene had to have been terrifying for Jo and Jenny. He could only imagine how difficult this must be for them. Kayakers seldom survive entrapment underwater for long. Air is essential for life, and after five minutes without oxygen, brain damage begins. Thinking and memory skills are the first to go. Without oxygen, a drowning victim may die or be left with permanent brain damage—if they survive. Watching a paddler disappear would be traumatic. As trip leaders, Will and Jo would assume major responsibility for the accident and be guilt ridden for the rest of their lives.

Though Kayden could not have known it, a frightening picture already haunted their minds. Several minutes after Kayden had disappeared under the rock, Will and Jo had spotted Kayden's kayak floating helplessly down the river, full of water with its bow pointing skyward. Fatal accidents often result in post-traumatic stress disorder for anyone who witnesses them. Survival guilt consumes their lives as they struggle to make sense of how such a tragedy could occur.

As he leaned against the cavern wall, Kayden imagined what the rescue attempt above him looked like. There would be a strong sense of urgency as a rescue plan was devised. Ropes would be gathered, and a search strategy created. Will and Jo would create the plan together—an all-out effort would be made to save him. Jenny and Mark were likely instructed to go seek help by following the trail back to their starting point on the river.

Will and Jo were awesome individuals, and Kayden had great confidence in their ability to save his life. Both were trained in swift-water rescue and carried the necessary gear to rescue kayakers from very bad situations. He knew they would do everything within their power to save him. But was it even possible? His situation was a worst-case scenario for any paddler. He had been forced under a large boulder and had not been seen for hours. To compound matters, he knew the weather was getting bad, and heavy rainfall was likely for the next two days. More water would

CHAPTER 6

create larger, more powerful rapids. This would make any type of rescue very difficult.

Kayden had been in bad situations before. He had learned to adapt, sometimes to life events he could have never imagined. In the face of trauma, Kayden had learned to persevere, to never give up, even when things seemed to be out of control. At times, his life had been clouded with darkness, and Kayden had wondered what options, if any, he had to make his life better. He had been learning the answers to these questions over time, and it had not been easy.

Kayden was often quiet and reflective, yet he loved people and making friends. He was also drawn to adults, especially three who had made a big and unexpected difference in his life. They had entered his life when he had needed them most, after he had endured what he had later learned was the hardest loss a child could experience. His life had been broken apart when he was eight; he had worked hard to put the pieces back together. His journey had been painful.

As Kayden leaned his back against the cavern wall, the fatigue of the day's events hit him. His eyelids became heavy, and his limbs felt numb. A combination of exhaustion, cold, and fear came down on him, and his mind drifted. His breathing became heavy and then slowed, and his head fell back against the wall. His eyes closed and began to dart from side to side. The dream returned, the one he dreaded most.

Chapter 7

"Rock bottom became the solid foundation on which
I rebuilt my life."

—J. K. Rowling (author of the Harry Potter books)

Kayden had experienced this dreadful dream many times in the past four years. It was vivid—and true to the smallest detail. It replayed in perfect sequence the day that his life had changed forever.

It was a Saturday morning and the phone rang, just like it had countless times. This time, however, was different. Shortly after Kayden's mom lifted the phone to her ear, Kayden saw the color drain from her face. The caller identified himself as a state trooper from South Carolina. Her gaze darted around the room, and her mouth drooped. Time appeared to slow, and Kayden watched his mom's lips moving.

"No, no, no, this cannot be!" she said, her head moving from side to side, and her hand tightened on the phone. There was a tremble in her voice. "You have the wrong person," she muttered. "My husband can't be dead. He can't be!"

Kayden stared in disbelief at what his mom was saying. He had never seen her act this way. Could this really be happening? His father, whom he had just hugged goodbye the day before, was gone? In shock, Kayden felt his stomach churn. A strong pressure developed behind his eyes as tears streamed down his cheeks. Perhaps this was all a bad dream, and surely he would awaken soon. His father, the man he loved beyond measure, was gone?

The woman behind the wheel of the Chevy Camaro that had struck his dad's car had been drunk, very drunk. As his dad had crested a hill on Interstate 85 near Greenville, South Carolina, her Camaro's headlights had appeared directly in front of him without warning. She had been driving on the wrong side of the interstate, heading southbound in the northbound lane for more than ten miles. It was unclear how she had entered the south-bound lane. Any attempt to avoid the collision would have been futile. Both cars had been traveling at sixty-five miles per hour as they topped the hill. The crash had been horrific. Glass and metal had exploded across all four lanes of the interstate, and in a chain reaction, eight additional vehicles had smashed into his dad's car, creating a fiery domino effect. Numerous vehicles had burst into flames on impact, and rescue vehicles had converged en masse at the site. The sound of rotor blades had filled the night sky as air-ambulance helicopters arrived and landed in the median. First responders had worked frantically to cut people from smoldering heaps of metal, ever mindful of the danger of explosions from ruptured fuel tanks. Kayden had learned from the paramedics that his dad had likely died on impact. All efforts to revive him had been unsuccessful.

The recurring nightmare continued to play out.

Kayden stood from the chair he'd been sitting on in the family room and walked numbly toward his mom. He thrust his arms out and hugged her as he never had before. He was afraid to let her go. He could feel her heart pounding, and his own heart ached. With tears still flowing down his cheeks, he looked up into his mother's eyes. Her gaze appeared distant and hopeless, one he had never seen before. He glanced away, his eyes shifting to the clock. It was 3:33 p.m., and the pendulum below the clockface continued to swing back and forth. This seemed odd to Kayden, who felt like the world had just stopped, frozen in time. He slowly let go of his mother, kissed her on the cheek, and moved across the family room to his father's chair. He stared at the blue recliner, and the memories rushed forward: his dad smiling as he watched football, his dad napping, his dad sitting and talking to him.

Wrestling.

Kayden's dad had been a wrestler in high school and college. He had enjoyed tussling with his son and helped him develop an interest in the sport. Two years after his father's death, Kayden had begun wrestling competitively, in part to honor his father's memory. His first year had been tough, and he had lost many of his matches. He had done better his second year, though, vastly improving his technique and strength. He had known that his father was smiling down on him at the end of his second season, when Kayden had battled his way to the finals of a midseason tournament and faced a regional champion. Kayden's opponent, who had garnered a sizable lead of ten to four going into the final period, had made several mocking comments during the match about Kayden's father dying. Kayden had been shocked by the cruel comments, but they had invoked an even stronger determination from deep within him. He had found *the zone.*

Kayden had maintained his focus and refused to give up. With one minute remaining, he had used his best move, a Granby roll, to reverse his opponent and turn him to his back. His startled opponent had been caught off guard, and Kayden had taken full advantage. Sensing victory, he had exerted every ounce of his strength and pinned his adversary with two seconds remaining in the final period. His coach and teammates had rushed the mat in jubilation. Even though Kayden's dad had been gone for two years, he had felt his presence with him during the match. It was his favorite memory, and he had dedicated his victory to his dad.

Paddling.

Kayden had received his first kayak when he was just six years old. The boat had been a surprise gift under the Christmas tree. The cockpit had been filled with several other presents: a life jacket, a paddle, and a helmet. This had been Kayden's best Christmas gift ever. His dad had been an avid outdoorsman and an experienced kayaker. During his college years, he had been president of the paddling club and had paddled the most challenging rivers in the eastern part of the United States. His dad had been a skilled teacher, and soon Kayden had joined him on the local lakes and calm rivers. He had been a quick learner and could soon maneuver his kayak with ease. They had joined a local paddling club and participated in several outings, including two overnight trips. Back then, Kayden's goal had been to paddle whitewater rivers with his dad when he got older. Kayden was thankful that his dad had been generous with his time and had often adjusted his work schedule to be with his son. Kayden cherished the memories of their trips together. Sitting around campfires and floating down rivers brought back many good memories. It had seemed easier to talk on the water and in the woods. He was not sure why.

Napping.

Kayden's father had worked hard and had often fallen asleep just moments after reclining in his chair. His dad had been special and loved by many, especially his family. There had been a magnetic quality about Mr. Barrett that had drawn friends and family close to him. He had been unpredictable and loved to laugh. His pranks had been a frequent source of amusement.

Kayden had often climbed into the recliner and snuggled down in the space between the arm of it and his dad, who had always reached around and pulled him in tight. This had been Kayden's safe place. He could feel the closeness of his dad whenever this memory entered his mind.

Kayden stepped back from the chair, his body trembling. In a mere instant, he realized that his safe zone was gone and would never return. His body trembled again, and this time his legs buckled; he fell to his knees. He began to sob like he had never sobbed before. The pain was intense; it felt like a knife had pierced his heart. Kayden pulled his knees tight to his chest and began to rock back and forth. He knew his life had changed forever. He was afraid the pain might never end.

Kayden had experienced this nightmare at least twice a month since his father had died. It was vivid in his memory even after he woke from it, and it served as a painful reminder of that day. He recalled the time immediately following his dad's death as a blur of people in and out of their home. Most of the visitors had been from their church and his school. All had been eager to help and had tried to comfort Kayden and his mom. Their offers of food and support had been nice and certainly well intended. However, often during the months after his dad's passing, Kayden had been overwhelmed by the number and frequency of visitors. At times, he had just wanted to be left alone and had found comfort in music, especially some of his dad's favorite songs. His father had been a gifted musician and had sung tenor in their church's praise band. Kayden had a CD of his dad performing several songs and often found relief in listening to it. He found it odd that he could hear his dad's voice but could no longer talk to him. That was painful, but the fact that his father's music would remain with him forever was reassuring.

The initial months and years after his dad's passing had been painful for Kayden. A variety of firsts had taken on a special meaning. The first Thanksgiving. The first Christmas. The first Easter. The first football game. All had been painful reminders of the way his life had changed. Nighttime was the worst. He would toss and turn as he tried to fall asleep. His biggest fear was *the dream* that paid him frequent visits. On some occasions, it would wake him up. His body would be covered in sweat and his heart racing. Night terrors were always the worst, and he wanted them to go away, never to return. He shared the dreams with his mom, even though he knew it was hard for her to hear.

Kayden had been surprised one Friday afternoon when his mom asked him to join her for ice cream at the local Dairy Queen. He loved Blizzards and was more than willing to go along for his favorite dessert. While waiting for their orders to be filled, his mom told Kayden that she had spoken recently with his fourth-grade teacher, Mrs. Pryor. Kayden's teacher had reported many positives about his effort, attitude, and grades in school. However, she had noticed his frequent sad expressions and tendency to stare out the window. Mrs. Pryor had also said there would be a grief group starting soon at his school for students who had experienced loss. The group would meet once a week during lunch breaks for eight weeks with the school's counselor and psychologist. Mrs. Pryor had thought it might be helpful for him. Kayden recalled his initial reaction: "No way!" His life had been quite different already, and he'd had no desire to be singled out further from his friends. Eventually, though, he had agreed to try the group with encouragement from his mom and teacher. He had grown tired of sleepless nights and the pain in his heart.

On the first day of his grief group meeting, Kayden had gathered his lunch tray and walked to the counselor's office. He was nervous but happy to have a slice of pepperoni pizza on his plate, one of his favorites. As Kayden entered the office, he was surprised to see two familiar faces—his friends Beau and Jay—along with three students he did not know. Four of the five students smiled at Kayden as he entered the room. He was greeted by the counselor, Mrs. McGhee, and a man he had seen around the school, Dr. Johnson. Kayden took a seat near the end of the table and settled into enjoying his pizza while looking around the office. There were posters with motivational quotes on the walls. He wondered what his friends Jay and Beau were doing there. Kayden had met Jay during a kayaking class a year earlier. He had a good sense of humor and often made Kayden laugh. Beau was a friend from his wrestling team; they often competed against each other. Kayden was very relieved to have both guys in his group.

The other three students were girls. He had seen them around school. Sarah was a new student, and her parents had divorced the previous year. Laura was a sixth grader whose brother had died in a car crash earlier in the school year. Cindy was in Kayden's grade and lived in foster care. Cindy's father was in prison, and her mom was addicted to drugs and lived on the streets in Atlanta. Cindy looked sad most of the time. Kayden could not recall a time he'd ever seen her smile. He had attempted to speak with her once, but she had only stared at him.

After everyone finished lunch, each student was asked to share one interesting fact about their life. Kayden was interested and listened carefully to each member of the group. He was surprised by their honesty. Jay went first. He was twelve years old and in the sixth grade. His mom had remarried the previous year. His father had taken his own life three years ago. *What?* Kayden thought. He'd had no idea that Jay's father had died.

Beau went next, pausing to look around at each group member. He was normally outgoing, but today his voice was soft. His eyes began to water as he spoke. Beau said his mom had left his family two years earlier. His dad was devastated, and Beau and his younger sister missed their mom terribly. Her leaving was such a shock for all of them. His dad had made an all-out effort to find her, but it had proved futile. Her last known location was on the West Coast, and she was reportedly living on the streets.

The girls went next. Sarah said she'd had to move the previous year after her parents divorced and her dad lost his job. She did not want to leave her old school and had tried to keep in touch with friends she had made while growing up. She was upset with her dad. He worked all the time and was not around much. She suspected that maybe he had a new girlfriend. After their divorce, Sarah's parents were hostile toward each other. She overheard her parents arguing on the phone late at night. Sarah tried to hide her pain and seldom talked about her family with her friends. She spent more and more time alone in her room and frequently cried herself to sleep.

Laura had a sad story as well. Her brother had died in a car accident at the beginning of the school year. He had been riding with a neighborhood friend to high school, and the teenager had been driving way too fast through their subdivision. The car hit a brick mailbox, and her brother had been ejected through the windshield. He had not been wearing his seat belt and died on the scene. He was her most trusted friend.

Cindy stared at Kayden before she spoke; it was as if she looked right through him. She said she had lived with both of her parents until three years ago when her dad was arrested for selling drugs. Cindy was not surprised since she seldom saw her father, and her mother said bad things about him—almost daily. Cindy's mom struggled and could not keep a job. When she left Cindy and her younger brother alone for three days, a neighbor reported her to social services. After a short investigation, Cindy and her brother were placed in foster care. Her foster family provided the best home Cindy and her brother had ever lived in, and she was slowly learning to trust her new family.

Kayden was shocked at what he heard from the others in the group. His heart ached for them, yet he also experienced an odd sense of relief. He had felt so very alone after his dad died. He had experienced a seemingly endless darkness, a profound sadness that he'd thought only he could understand. Now, he realized that if anyone could understand what he had been through, it was the five other members in his group. For the first time since his dad died, he was not alone in his pain. Several of his friends had experienced more anguish and hardship than he had—and somehow survived. As Dr. Johnson and Mrs. McGhee summarized what they had heard from each student, Kayden found himself looking forward to their next meeting.

The next seven sessions were a blur. Kayden found himself eager to meet with his group each week. It was spring; the school year would be over in eight more weeks. A strong bond had developed between the six students in the group that was unlike any friendships Kayden had experienced before. With each meeting, they learned more about the incredible hardships they'd endured. Their grief was real, yet their tears were often accompanied by laughter. Kayden found this odd, but he liked it.

Cindy said very little during the first two meetings, but Kayden saw her smile twice. By the third meeting she began to share her story. Kayden watched her change each week as she became more comfortable with her new friends. Cindy's life was full of tragedy, and her story just flowed. Her anguish was real, and Kayden began to understand why she looked numb during their first meeting. She connected with Kayden and soon began talking to him in the hallways and at lunch. He enjoyed her friendship.

Kayden was shocked during their fifth meeting when he unexpectedly began to cry. As his sorrow washed over him, he described what his dad had meant to him growing up and was thankful that his friends just listened. He missed his dad more than he could imagine. At the end of their meeting, Cindy walked slowly toward him, her arms open. She gave him a hug and turned away without saying a word. She did not need to. A bond stronger than any glue had developed among the group members. For Kayden, it seemed like a new family.

Dr. Johnson and Mrs. McGhee were great listeners and good at helping them share their darkest moments. They also shared practical ways for surviving and growing through life's toughest challenges. Kayden needed their help. After his dad died, he knew his life was out of control. His dad really could not be gone, could he? Kayden could still hear his voice and see every detail in his face. He would wake up crying and be unable to shake the sadness in his soul. At other times, he was angry at the world and everyone in it. Why did *his* dad have to die? He missed him more than anything and often thought about ways he could bring him back. He was more than willing to make a deal, any deal, if he could see his dad again, even if only for a few minutes. At times, Kayden's pain was unbearable, and his mind was filled with darkness. As he struggled to understand his pain, Kayden was surprised to hear an inner voice begin to whisper that he would be okay, that he would find a way through the pain. This voice became stronger as he heard about the painful events his friends in the grief group had experienced.

During their sixth meeting, Dr. Johnson started by explaining that grief affects everyone differently, but there are some common experiences most people have.

"Grief is like ocean waves breaking along the shore," Dr. Johnson said. "It comes and goes, and some waves are stronger than others." He took a deep breath and continued, "There are normal reactions to grief, like denial."

Kayden's mind raced back to the day of the phone call from the state trooper. He recalled his disbelief at what he had heard.

Dr. Johnson shared that anger was also a common reaction to loss. Kayden knew this all too well; he was furious that his dad had left. What Dr. Johnson said about bargaining with grief also made sense; Kayden would do anything if he could bring his dad back. He was not surprised to learn that depression would be part of his journey through grief. This one he expected. Kayden was encouraged to learn that the quiet voice he heard within himself was normal. He would find a way to accept the loss of his dad even though he did not like it, nor could he change it. Kayden felt better knowing that his friends had gone through experiences similar to his. He no longer felt alone.

On the last day, Mrs. McGhee shared a memorable message: "You grow through what you go through!" The grief group had provided fertile soil in which to grow. Kayden realized that his hurt, anger, and confusion were not only common but also normal. The term *resiliency* was also emphasized; Kayden liked the concept. His takeaway was that everyone encounters hard times and has to be ready to roll with the changes of life. This sounded good to Kayden, but how to do it was complicated. All he could do was try.

Chapter 8

"Do not give up. The beginning is always the hardest."

—Kemmy Nola

The water slowly rose in the cavern. Kayden had slumped back against the wall when he had fallen asleep. Water had slowly crept over his lips and entered his mouth. He gagged as it slid down his throat. The recurring dream ended as quickly as it had begun. Kayden's body shook from the nightmare and the cold river water. As his mind began to clear, he anxiously leaped to his feet.

How long had he slept? Kayden remembered the weather forecast had called for rain and possibly heavy thunderstorms in the afternoon. The Opa River was known for flash flooding. This could prove disastrous. If the river level rose more than two feet, the remaining air inside the cave would be slowly pushed out by the water, and he would drown. He fought a pending sense of doom. If he panicked, he would die.

"No matter how difficult the circumstance, there is always an answer to your problem," Dr. Johnson had said. He'd reinforced the comment during grief group sessions with several powerful stories of survival, and it had stuck with Kayden. Even in the worst circumstances, there are always alternatives to explore. He would never give up.

Kayden forced himself to take three deep breaths and think about his options. What could he do? Exactly how bad was his situation? Kayden knew he had to see his surroundings in order to plan. Light, he needed light! He pulled the watertight canister of matches from his life jacket. He carefully unscrewed the top and retrieved one match from the cylinder and struck it. A sudden radiance filled the cavern as the light displaced the darkness. The water in the cavern was continuing to rise, faster than he thought possible. More alarming was the swirl of currents not far from his seat against the wall. The additional water made the vortex much stronger. He could feel the strength of the rotating water, power in the darkness, drawing him toward the center of the vortex. He pressed his back firmly against the wall with his feet. This held him in place for now.

As the flame slowly burned down the match, Kayden shifted his gaze toward the top of the cave. He was alarmed at what he saw. The space between the swirling waters of the vortex and the top of the cavern was little more than two feet. There had been at least three feet of space before he passed out from exhaustion. This was confirmation of what he feared most. The river would soon fill the cavern, and he would be out of options. Kayden needed an escape plan. He reached for another match and struggled to keep his hands from shaking. As the match lit, Kayden again surveyed his surroundings. The vortex was gaining strength as the water continued to rise. He scanned every nook of the walls surrounding him. Was there any way of escape?

Once again, Kayden took three deep breaths and tried to calm himself. He studied his surroundings. He looked up, down, and all around his watery world. The walls were quickly disappearing as water filled the cave. With his heart racing, Kayden tipped his head back and gazed upward, the one direction that frightened him most. There, he finally found a ray of hope. The rock directly above him was indented, leaving additional space, maybe two feet. Over thousands of years, the water had entered the chasm and slowly eroded the rock. The composition above Kayden's head was less dense and had been worn away, leaving a cone-shaped indentation that would provide additional space for him to breathe—and hopefully survive.

Kayden's mind started to race. He could not let panic win. He had goals, and despite his painful childhood, he enjoyed life. He had to find a way out. Was there anything he had not considered? His forehead ached as he tried to think of alternatives. He shifted his hands from his waist to his chest to ensure his eleven remaining matches were safe inside the canister. As he did so, his hand brushed against the other pocket of his life jacket. His left pocket had contained his safety matches, and the right one contained another object he had somehow missed. Inside the pocket was a soft plastic case that held a folded survival blanket. His dad had given him the shiny foil thermal blanket on his eighth birthday. It was compact and made of a bright reflective material. This was an essential part of a kayaker's safety gear and could be used to help a paddler retain warmth. Kayden was excited to have another tool to help him in his battle to survive! The icy water in the cavern was taking its toll on Kayden. He carefully unwrapped the blanket and placed it around his body. He had to conserve what little body heat he had left.

Kayden paused and continued to take deep breaths. One thought repeatedly crossed his mind: his friends were resourceful and would do everything within their power to save him. But how? River rescues are complicated and require careful planning by individuals trained in swift-water rescue techniques. It is vital to know where the person was last seen and if any obstructions may have trapped the individual underwater. Rescue efforts are more difficult during storm conditions, especially if heavy rainfall causes a flash flood. Large objects such as cars, trucks, and animals are often swept away and found miles from their original location.

Kayden contemplated this dilemma as he leaned against the back of the cavern. He was tired, and his body was beginning to ache. He shivered from the cold, and a familiar dull pressure existed in his abdomen; his bladder was full. Kayden sighed as the water warmed slightly around him. Any form of heat was helpful at this point, regardless of where it came from. As Kayden considered his options, his helmet scraped against the back of the wall. The noise startled him, and he jerked his head forward. His helmet! Kayden had learned the importance of wearing a helmet and had never ventured down a river without it. Kayakers were most at risk after flipping since their head could strike rocks. A helmet protected the paddler from being knocked unconscious if his head struck an object while underwater.

Kayden's helmet was bright yellow and could not be missed. It served as a visual beacon to his location on the river. An all-important plan began to form, and a grin spread across his face in the darkness. Would it work? Could this be the answer to him escaping? Kayden reached in his pockets and carefully removed the matches and his knife. It was time to put his plan into action.

Chapter 9

*"When you have exhausted all possibilities,
remember this: you haven't."*

—Thomas A. Edison

Jo stared at the rescue scene along the banks of the Opa River. It was frenzied and chaotic. A line of thunderstorms had descended quickly with heavy rain that made visibility difficult. As the thunder echoed through the river valley, she watched frequent lightning strikes light up the forested banks of the river. The trees bent as wind gusts exceeded thirty miles per hour, driving the rain into horizontal sheets of water. The conditions could not have been worse for a river rescue. Jo turned her head away from a powerful gust of wind and rain. As she turned her head, she detected a group of paddlers, barely visible as they rounded the bend of the river near where Kayden had disappeared. This section of the river was strewn with large boulders that prevented them from beaching their kayaks and seeking refuge from the storm.

"Look, we have company coming our way," Jo yelled to Will as she pointed in their direction. Jo and Will lifted their paddles in unison and waved them back and forth. Both blew hard into their whistles attached to their life jackets. The shrill sounds carried into the distance against the frequent rumbles of thunder.

The group consisted of four kayakers. The lead paddler understood the urgency after hearing the frequent whistles and seeing the rapid paddle motions, a commonly agreed upon sign of distress among paddlers. He turned his head back toward his group, no doubt affirming a crisis ahead. Immediately, all four paddlers accelerated their pace, the bows of their kayaks slicing through the waters of the Opa River at full speed. Jo noticed a smoothness in their paddle strokes, a strong indicator that the group on the way were not novices. She was encouraged by what she saw.

The group leader reached the rock first. He beached his kayak and directed his three friends to a smooth landing spot near where Jo and Will were standing. The paddlers approached Will and Jo, their brows furrowed with concentration. The leader was clearly an experienced kayaker who finessed his boat with skill and power as he approached the landing spot. He introduced himself as David, a faculty member of a local university and sponsor of the university's kayaking club to which the others in his group belonged. All six huddled together as Will described the accident scene loudly over the roar of the wind and the frequent clap of thunder. Each kayaker knew exactly what was at stake, and Will was extremely grateful for the additional support.

After describing the accident, Will led the team to the spot where Kayden had last been seen. Jo described the moment the throw rope hit Kayden's hands and how he had been unable to hang on. Her lips quivered as she described how Kayden had disappeared under the rock, vanishing right before her eyes. Will looked at David and the others who had just joined the rescue operation. Their expressions were somber and focused. What, if any, chance was there of finding Kayden alive?

David posed a key question. "How long has Kayden been missing?"

The question hung in the air, creating an awkward and painful silence. Will glanced at his watch and then looked directly at David as he replied, "Three hours." Their efforts to find Kayden had been exhausting, and their sense of time had been compromised. Three hours was a long time, and the river had continued to rise.

Will's answer was not what any of the new rescuers wanted to hear. Experienced kayakers know the realities and dangers of paddling whitewater rivers. Entrapment underwater is the worst-case scenario, and after fifteen minutes, a rescue mission ultimately turns into a recovery mission. The return of a body at least provides some closure for a family dealing with the stark realization that their loved one has died. Will's and Jo's stomachs tightened, and their mouths filled with saliva from the waves of nausea sweeping through their bodies. They could not bear the thought of recovering Kayden's body and returning to tell his mom.

Reid, one of the new arrivals, listened intently to Jo and Will, then surveyed his surroundings and left the group. He jumped to a small ledge just above the entrance rapid where Kayden had disappeared. Reid's movements among the rocks were fluid and smooth, a skill that he had developed over the past ten years as an avid rock climber and instructor.

Reid had assisted in recovering an injured climber off a rock wall two years before. The group of climbers was more than

1,000 feet up on a vertical rock wall when a rock the size of a softball broke loose from under the lead climber and struck the climber in the second position, knocking him unconscious. Even though the climber had a helmet on, the impact left him motionless on the wall; he had to be rescued and lowered to the ground. The lead climber led a coordinated and efficient rescue effort. Reid assisted in setting up the belay system to lower their friend to safety. Once off the rock wall, the rescued climber slowly regained consciousness and was transported to the local hospital. He suffered a major concussion that required him to refrain from climbing for the next year. Although he was not in charge of the rescue effort, Reid gained valuable experience and confidence from the incident.

An enthusiastic outdoorsman, Reid had recently taken a course in swift-water rescue from a local outdoor center. As an engineering student, he was fascinated by the dynamics of moving water and, more importantly, how to extract paddlers from dangerous situations. He enjoyed the course and equipped his kayak with the suggested rescue equipment along with a few additional items: a small pulley, a climbing harness, extra carabiners, and a small, movable sling of rope known as a prusik. Reid was amazed at the simplicity and compactness of his rescue bag tucked behind the seat of his kayak. He had hoped he would never have to use it.

Reid had more experience on the Opa River than any of the other paddlers. On a trip the previous year, he had paddled the river in late summer at low water. The group had to get out of their kayaks and carry them around several rapids because there was not enough water to float their boats. Reid got an up-close look at the various rock formations that made the rapids on the Opa River so challenging. He had been most fascinated by the very spot where Kayden had disappeared. He clearly recalled the undercut boulders and unusual makeup of the rocks on this rapid. His interest was also piqued by his background in geology. Knowledge of rocks, water, and physics was a near-perfect background for a paddler and rock climber. Reid hoped his expertise could help in this emergency.

He jumped back from the ledge and rejoined the group. His agile nature caught the attention of those watching him.

"I was on this river last year and saw this area at low water," Reid told the group. "This entrance rapid leads into a series of undercut rocks that create small caverns. Large objects have disappeared here and not flushed through. There is a chance that Kayden is trapped in one of the small caverns." Reid turned his head upward toward the darkening clouds and then shifted his attention to the different formations along the bank. His tone was serious as he spoke: "The major problem is that the river is rising quickly. We need to move fast to find Kayden."

A plan was forming in Reid's mind, one that he had learned in his swift-water rescue course. The main flow of the river was channeling into the area where Kayden was likely trapped. The water needed to be diverted, a daunting task to say the least. Redirecting rivers often requires massive equipment, and that was not an option for the group. Reid was a persistent and creative person. He liked to solve problems. No matter how difficult the situation, he approached every challenge with a passion and deter-mination that astonished those around him. As he surveyed the boulders, Reid knew he had to somehow block the flow of water entering the cave. There was a log just above the entrance, and Kayden had barely made it underneath it before he disappeared into the Room of Doom. Reid's strategy began to formulate in his mind, and his confidence began to build. He blew his whistle and waved for everyone to join him. The plan had to be carefully executed with precision and teamwork. An ominous air hung over the group. Each minute that passed lowered the possibility that Kayden would be found alive. It was now or never.

Chapter 10

"When you come to the end of your rope,
tie a knot and hang on."

—Franklin D. Roosevelt

Kayden's situation inside the cavern was desperately deteriorating. He shivered from the cold as he extracted his
knife from the pocket of his life jacket. His wrinkled fingers fumbled at the slot used to access the blade. The dark and cold
conditions did not help. The numbness in his fingers made this
typically easy task difficult.

Kayden reached for his matches and unscrewed the lid. Fifteen
seconds of light was plenty to open the blade and survey his
surroundings. As he struck the match, the flame momentarily
flickered before shining on the dripping gray and black rock walls
around him. He was startled by what he saw. The water in the
cave had risen by six more inches. He glanced overhead, preparing himself for what he might see. His heart sank at the sight.
He estimated about eighteen inches of headroom remained. The
water was flowing in much quicker than it exited. At this rate, the

remaining space would be filled in the next four to six hours. Or would it? Kayden knew the Opa River was prone to flash flooding. Perhaps the drainage was also fast?

Kayden made another alarming discovery. The pressure around his waist and torso had increased, and he found himself exerting more effort to keep his body back against the wall. This required additional strength, a precious resource that was slowly slipping away. He knew why that was happening but did not want to think about it. The vortex. As the match grew dimmer, Kayden saw that the swirling vortex in the center of the cavern had expanded to almost twice the size it had been before. The water flow was pulling Kayden toward the center, beckoning him toward a terrifying end to his twelve-year life. As he fought it, he realized that the force that was trying to kill him could end up saving his life.

He shoved his body against the wall of the cave to minimize the forces drawing him toward a watery death. Light, he needed light for the next step of his plan. He struck another match and closely scanned his shrinking space. The whirlpool was wider, steeper, and stronger. A gurgling sound emerged from the bowels of the vortex as the water strived to escape through the constricted passage. When the flame was halfway down the stick, he reached for his knife and helmet. He examined the helmet carefully. It was made from a strong yellow plastic and had foam inserts for comfort and protection. Kayden had experimented with his helmet on a previous river trip to see if it would float. He remembered a sense of relief when he slowly released the helmet from his hands and it remained above water, but barely. This would make it easier to find if it ever floated away by accident.

The helmet and knife were central to his escape. He had to deliver a message to his friends who were trying to locate and rescue him. His plan was well conceived, but would it work? He carefully inspected his knife and touched the tip of the blade. The knife was new, and the tip was very sharp. It was the ideal tool to carve his message. Kayden placed the knife in his teeth and grasped his helmet in both hands. He rubbed his hands over the helmet, searching for the largest surface area. The back of the helmet worked the best and would be the perfect location for his message. In the dark and foreboding cavern, Kayden placed the helmet in his left hand and took the knife from his mouth with his right hand. He pressed the tip of the knife into the left side of the back of his helmet and dragged the knife blade down. Next, he completed a horizontal line followed by an additional vertical line. There, his first letter was completed! The letter H was roughly shaped but should be recognizable. The next letter required one vertical line and three horizontal markings. The letter E. The third letter was easier and consisted of just one vertical and one horizontal line to create the letter L. The final letter was the most difficult. He made the vertical line for the P and struggled to make the loop.

Drained from the tedious carving, he reached for another match, desperately hoping his message was legible. He unscrewed the cap and fumbled for a match. As the light pierced the darkness, Kayden examined the back of his helmet. The word was irregular and somewhat misshapen, but legible! The letters were clearly etched in the plastic, and anyone who located the helmet would readily see the simple message carved into the back of the helmet: H-E-L-P. It would let the rescuers know that Kayden was alive and ensure that an all-out effort would be made to rescue—not recover—him.

Now he needed a means to send it. The vortex. Could he use the dark and menacing whirlpool that was attempting to pull him into a deadly underworld for good? The spinning downward currents would be powerful enough to pull his helmet into the vortex. Its relatively small size and minimal buoyancy increased the chance that it would flush out of the cavern. Once free, the bright yellow helmet would slowly float to the surface and be located by a member of the rescue team. This was Kayden's best and probably only chance, and he knew it.

Kayden struck another match. As the cavern began to glow, he could see the water level had risen several more inches. He looked directly above his head and was terrified to see the ceiling of the cave appeared to be drawing closer. He saw the center of the vortex about ten feet away and figured that was where he needed to toss his helmet. As the match burned halfway down, he took three careful steps in the direction of the vortex. The water pulled harder than ever before, drawing his body toward the center. Kayden was in a tug of war that he had to win! His reaction was immediate. He pitched his helmet toward the center of the vortex and leaned back, using his legs to drive his body toward the safety of the wall. As the light from the match faded, he saw his helmet land in the middle of the vortex and disappear as the downward suction of the water pulled it from sight. He felt his feet slip across the slimy rocks as he forced himself against the wall, trying to flatten his back to gain every inch of distance possible from the power of the vortex. He was exhausted and gasping for air. He knew that unless the waters started to recede, he would only have air for another hour—at the most.

Despite his grim situation, Kayden was relieved he had put his plan into action. He hoped that it would be enough to save him. He was unwilling to let his life end this way. He had to take control to survive. His desire to live remained stronger than ever for many reasons. Most of all, he yearned to see his mom and Jenny. With absolutely no strength left, he leaned back against the wall and prepared himself for whatever would come next. He knew he had to be ready.

Chapter 11

"Disappointment always arrives before hope and the darkness of night comes before the dawn. Don't lose hope now because things will be brighter with the new day."

—Henry Rollins

Jo watched Reid carefully as he kneeled in the middle of the group of rescuers and used a stick in the sand to outline his rescue plan. Will and the other paddlers leaned in as Reid drew a simple diagram of the entrance to the rapid where Kayden had disappeared.

It was shaped like a funnel, wide at the top and narrow near the bottom. The location where Kayden vanished under the rock was about eight feet wide. The water foamed and boiled as it slammed into the large boulder. Reid likened it to fifty fire hoses trained on a boulder at close range. Spray and mist hung in the air, and the sound was like a small jet engine at full power. The ground vibrated from the energy of the water slamming into the large rocks, a turbulence that defies description.

The force of the water entering the sieve-like rapid needed to be stopped. The fallen tree was a key element to the plan. If the idea worked as Reid had conceived it, a small dam would be placed just beneath the tree and boulder, allowing the water to be redirected away from where Kayden had disappeared. The action would require careful implementation, and small details mattered. Reid had carefully assessed the resources needed for creating a small dam. He needed an object about nine feet long and four feet wide. More importantly, the object had to be light enough to maneuver into the precise spot on the river. There were numerous logs of varied sizes along the riverbank. Reid speculated these were too heavy and cumbersome to move, even for this group of strong, well-conditioned paddlers. He scanned the surroundings for anything that could be used to redirect the movement of water. The structure would need to be built from materials that were strong enough to change the flow of the river yet light enough to maneuver by hand. A sense of frustration took hold as Reid searched for natural objects that could be used.

As he continued searching, the bright red color of his own kayak caught his eye. Of course! The solution was right in front of him, and there was not just one but two kayaks. The length of his boat was just under ten feet and would fit into the channel perfectly. The boat was also light and easily maneuvered by just two people. The key would be to place the kayak exactly into the opening of the slot and wedge it between the tree and the rock. The force of the water would pin the craft in place and shift the flow to the left. Once the flow of the water was diverted, it might be possible to access the spot where Kayden was last seen.

Reid surveyed the group and took a stick into his hand. Jo's eyes were transfixed as he drew an outline of the rapid. The center of the drawing featured the large boulder where Kayden had disappeared. The fallen tree and boulder were just upriver from where the flow of the river channeled into an eight-foot-wide chute. Reid's plan was clear in his mind, and he knew that execution would be the key. Success would require that each member of his team followed his directions exactly. Reid had determined Will to be a skilled and attentive leader whom he could rely on to implement his idea. He also had great respect for his friend and trip leader David. Reid chose David to help him construct the dam and had confidence that his friend knew exactly how to redirect the flow of water away from the cave. Will and David had watched Reid intently as he had finished drawing his plan in the sand.

Reid collected his rescue bag from his kayak. As he returned to the group, a bolt of lightning shot down from a dark cloud above, striking a tree less than a mile away. The ground shook from the thunder only two seconds after the flash. Reid could not help but notice the flow of the river had increased again. Conditions for putting the rescue plan into action had gone from bad to worse.

Reid tied a rescue rope to the front and back of his kayak and asked David and Will to listen carefully. "Let's create a dam with one, possibly two kayaks, which we will lower on ropes," Reid shouted over the roar of the storm. "As we lower the boats slowly, the cockpits will fill. The force of water will wedge the kayaks between the tree and boulder, creating a dam. Will, I want you to handle the rope from across the river. David and I will handle the line on this side."

Will sprinted in the rain up the windy path to the spot Reid described. Reid and David moved quickly to their location, each carrying one end of the kayak. Reid coiled the bow line so that he could throw it the ten feet across the river to Will. His throw had to be accurate to ensure Will could catch the rope. As Reid released the line, the wind intensified, and Will had to reach out over the river to grab the rope. He removed the slack to ensure the line was taut. He confidently looked Reid and David in the eye and nodded to indicate that he was ready. Together, they lowered the kayak until it was just above the surface of the rapid. As the bottom of the boat touched the turbulent water, the boat bounced slightly upward. This created a small pendulum effect. The rescuers needed to coordinate their efforts to place it in the precise spot. Timing was critical. As the suspended kayak swung forward toward the boulders, Will, David, and Reid lowered it. The force of the water filled the inside and forced the kayak down between two boulders perfectly! The position was at a slight angle, shifting the force of the water down a small chute between two rocks. The kayak was submerged and obstructed most, but not all, of the flow. David carefully inspected the makeshift dam and considered his options. There was less water flowing into the cavern, but was it enough for the rescuers to enter? If the kayak shifted, the water would immediately return to the main flow and jeopardize the rescuers attempting to reach Kayden in the cave.

Without hesitation, Reid told David to bring his kayak over to create a larger and stronger dam. By stacking two kayaks, Reid thought the dam would divert the entire flow and make the rescue safer and easier. David retrieved his kayak and secured lines to the bow and stern. They repeated the same process, and the second kayak was soon secured on top of the first one. The team had worked well together. Both boats were under tremendous force as the water level continued to rise on the Opa. Although the placement was ideal, Reid was not entirely confident the improvised dam would hold. The power generated by moving water was immense, and he feared the kayaks were close to their structural limits. If they folded, the waters would immediately return to their original path and flood the cavern where Kayden was likely trapped. The rescuers would be unable to escape and likely drown. As Reid observed the entrance, only a small stream continued to flow under the rock.

The next step was clear and dangerous. The entrance to the cave was accessible now and just large enough to enter. Who would be willing to go into the dark and narrow cave? Would anyone? Time was of the essence, and every delay placed Kayden's life at greater risk. Will, David, Jo, and Reid all stared at the small entrance. At the same time, the group diverted their gaze from the cavern and eyed each other. The team nodded in unison as David lifted the rescue rope. It was time.

The passage was now accessible, but what hazards loomed under the boulder? Water was still entering the cave and could entrap the rescuers in the narrow entrance. The roar of the river was a constant as the group considered their options. David slowly lowered his rescue bag and curiously pointed up near the top of the mountain. He'd seen a person he did not recognize. A petite and agile runner was hurtling down the trail, maintaining a frantic pace. As the runner neared the riverbank, Jo realized that Jenny had returned. She was leaping across boulders toward a location near the center of the river. Will scanned farther up the ridge, searching for any sign of Mark.

The team studied Jenny's movements from afar. She appeared to be determined to reach a certain location on the river. They watched intently as she approached a gap between two large boulders near the center of the river and leaned into it. What was she doing? Each member of the group stared, fearful to divert their hopeful gaze as Jenny disappeared between the rocks. Time stood still and an air of finality fell on the group. After what seemed like an eternity, she appeared carrying a round yellow object and ran toward them, closing the distance at a rate no one thought possible. But had Jenny been able to find a cell signal? Was help on the way?

Chapter 12

"Just because something isn't happening for you right now,
doesn't mean it will never happen . . ."

—Nicky Gumbel

The water continued to rise in the cavern, and the space above Kayden's head was disappearing. As water gradually displaced the air, he tilted his head back to provide easier access to the air within the six inches of space still available. As the water rose higher, he had to stand on tiptoe to keep his head above the surface. His breathing had increased along with his heart rate. He forced himself to steady his breathing, occasionally taking deep gulps of air and slowly exhaling. His options were very limited. He decided to remain with his back against the wall, trapped by the vortex, and hope and pray that he would be rescued in time by his friends. Maintaining calm was becoming increasingly difficult as he fought back the fear that was building in his mind. He could not and would not panic. Doing so would ensure the end, and he would drown. If the water continued to rise, the remaining oxygen would be slowly forced from the cavern and he would no longer be able to breathe. He had to escape. Somehow, he would find a way out.

Kayden had listened intently when he took his initial whitewater-paddling clinic. Will had explained a variety of ways to escape dangerous situations. Some of the options were far more appealing than others. One of the least appealing options was to remove one's life jacket and swim downward to escape the circular swirl of a hydraulic or vortex. This was the last option and should only be considered when all other options had failed.

The vortex had continued to strengthen within the cavern. The tug on Kayden's body was increasing, and fatigue was starting to show. Should he remove his life jacket and swim toward the center of the vortex? Kayden pondered his options: Was it possible he could be pulled down into the vortex and flushed out of the cavern? Would his body fit through the labyrinth of underwater passages? Without his life jacket, his body would be more likely to pass through. Was this even a possibility? How far would he have to swim blindly, feeling his way out with only his hands? Could he hold his breath long enough to survive?

As Kayden considered his desperate situation, he forced himself to remain focused. He had only two options. In Kayden's mind, neither plan seemed fair or desirable. Removing his life jacket and attempting to swim out through the vortex terrified Kayden, but it had to be considered. He decided to strike another match. Although the flame would burn some of his precious remaining oxygen, Kayden had to see if there were any other alternatives. As he lit the match, the glow revealed a solid rock ceiling above his head and swirling currents all around his body. It seemed more difficult to keep his body angled away from the vortex. The swirling waters lifted his body as he tried to remain wedged against the wall.

CHAPTER 12

Kayden's sense of time blurred as cold water and exhaustion dulled his senses. His eyelids became heavy, and he struggled to remain conscious. He turned his back one final time and pushed hard against the wall. A decision had to be made, and both choices were terrifying. As the match burned down and the heat started to warm his finger, he made a startling observation. Or did he? Was it an illusion? Visual hallucinations are not uncommon in desperate survival situations. Extreme exhaustion impairs the body and the brain. He had to take another look. As he reached for the match case in the pocket of his life jacket, he felt his remaining rescue tools, the whistle and knife. He did not want to leave his life jacket and remaining safety tools behind in a final desperate act to survive.

Another match. He had to know what was happening in the cave. As he struck the tip, the light revealed a change. The water level had dropped several inches in just the last few minutes! What had happened? How was it possible? The water level had been steadily increasing, and Kayden was acutely aware that his pocket of air was diminishing—until now! His brain released endorphins, survival chemicals that provided energy and clarity of mind. Would the water level continue to drop, or was this just a temporary break before a final surge filled the cavern? If the water continued to rise, he would be forced to cast himself into the vortex. He shuddered at the thought. If the water level continued to drop, his rescuers might be able to reach him. He thrust his back toward the groove in the cavern wall; he noticed it was slightly easier to wedge his body in place. Heartened by his discovery, Kayden clenched the match canister in his hand. He knew the matches were key to his survival; he did not want to let go.

After allowing several minutes to lapse, Kayden again reached into his case and took out another match. As the light pierced the darkness, Kayden's spirits lifted, and a sense of relief filled his body. The evidence was undeniable. The water level had dropped several more inches; he now had more than a foot of precious air above his head. Kayden was unable to control his excitement and screamed, "Yes!" The affirmation echoed loudly off the cavern wall. This was the first positive development since Mark had leaped onto the back of Kayden's kayak! On this fateful river trip, Kayden's circumstances had continued to deteriorate, in a series of disastrous events that tested his ability to survive. He was immensely thankful to be alive. Kayden's dad had sometimes called him strong willed, and he had been right.

Kayden knew that something about his situation had changed for the better. His confidence began to grow, and he sensed that help was not far away. As he thought about what to do next, he decided that his best course of action was no action. He would conserve his energy and wait for a rescue team to reach him. His last glimpse at the vortex was etched in his mind as his body shook in the cold water. Swimming into the swirling currents of the vortex to escape was no longer an option, for now. He felt a sense of relief and was grateful for the rescue efforts underway above him, likely only a few hundred feet from his location. He was able to breathe a sigh of relief as he thought about his yellow helmet disappearing into the vortex, destination unknown.

Chapter 13

"The best view comes after the hardest climb."

—Author Unknown

Jenny was fleet of foot, one of the fastest runners in her grade. After completing her 911 call, she began to backtrack down the mountain. The trails were steep, rocky, and slippery with occasional fallen trees blocking the way. Her water shoes frequently lost traction. At times, she slid down sections of the trail, as her mud-covered soles served more as skis than shoes. Jenny was determined to return to the river as quickly as she could. She was relieved to know that a rescue team was on the way. She was also very worried about Kayden and feared the worst. His death was an unbearable thought and weighed heavily on her mind. Her normally optimistic outlook was being tested by a harsh reality. After all, Kayden had disappeared under a large boulder during a terrible thunderstorm and had not been seen for hours. What possible chance did he have of surviving?

As Jenny sprinted down the trail, she thought back to the last time she had seen Mark. The memory was haunting. In full protective mode, the large mother bear had pounced on him, totally blocking Jenny's view of him. The animal's movements were powerful and swift as she attacked Mark's helpless body. Jenny shuddered at the grisly sight, knowing there was a good possibility that Mark had not survived the mauling. Bear attacks are rare but not unheard of in remote regions of the Appalachian Mountains. Mark's screams had faded slowly as she sprinted toward the top of the mountain ridge in search of a cell signal to call for help.

The final half mile back to the river was steep. Jenny was forced to slow her pace and regain her focus. As the path switched back and forth down the mountain, she remembered seeing one spot with a clear view of the river. She slowed her gait and cautiously approached the overlook with a sharp drop-off. Jenny made sure to stay several feet back from the dangerous cliff. She did not want to add to the list of victims on this disastrous trip.

Jenny scanned the river from two hundred feet above. Her observation point provided a view of the area just below Hell's Gate and the Room of Doom. She realized this vantage point would provide a panoramic view of the river downstream. Her eyes darted back and forth across the waterway, searching anxiously for any sign of Kayden. The raging waters continued to flow at a very past pace, producing a menacing sound that cut through the entire valley.

Jenny continued to search for Kayden, scanning the area with more intensity than she had ever searched for anything in her thirteen years of life. As her eyes tracked farther down the riverbed, she detected a small yellow object lodged between two rocks, about five hundred feet from the spot where Kayden had vanished. The object disappeared and reappeared as the waters churned between the two rocks. What was it? Jenny's heart sank as she recalled Kayden smiling at the beginning of the trip, his long blond hair protruding from the back of his bright yellow helmet.

Jenny grimaced with heartbreak as she cried out, "No, no, this cannot be happening!" Her conclusion was obvious. The bright yellow helmet marked the spot where Kayden had drowned, and his body was lodged between two big boulders. She could not bear the thought of his death. Her mind shifted into automatic mode, and she ran as fast as she could down the trail toward the river. The trees and rocks of the forest blurred; her mind was hyperfocused on the terrain ahead of her as she sought to avoid any detail that might slow her progress toward finding Kayden. As she approached the final eighth of a mile, she lost her footing on a forty-five-degree corner and slid more than thirty feet, tumbling down the side of the mountain. She used her feet to fend off the large rocks, and her fall was stopped by a boulder at the bottom. Scraped and bruised, she sprang to her feet and continued racing in the direction of the rocks where she had seen Kayden's helmet bobbing in the water. As she drew closer, she noticed a group of paddlers huddled together, just above the spot where Kayden had disappeared.

Jenny navigated a perilous approach across the tops of the rocks in the river toward the spot where Kayden's helmet was lodged. Her feet hopped from one boulder to the next as the bright yellow helmet loomed closer. When she reached the gap in the boulders, she glanced downward, preparing herself for the grim sight of Kayden's lifeless body. The top of the yellow helmet was lodged just below the surface, and Jenny fully expected to see Kayden's long blond hair flowing from underneath it in the current. As she kneeled for a closer look, a sudden immense feeling of relief spread throughout her body. It was only Kayden's helmet! So where was he? Could he still be alive?

Jenny reached down into the crevice, ever mindful not to fall into the narrow slot from which streams of water pulsated. She needed to retrieve Kayden's helmet. The protective inner foam was missing; presumably the harsh forces of the water had torn it free. As she lifted the helmet for closer examination, she made a heart-stopping discovery! She immediately wiped the tears from her eyes and reexamined what she thought she had seen. Sure enough, her eyes had not deceived her. She carefully ran her fingers over the four letters etched into the back of the helmet: H-E-L-P. How could this be? Was it possible that Kayden was still alive, after all this time, after the raging waters drove him underneath a large boulder?

Jenny paused and reflected. If Kayden were still alive, he would have to be trapped somewhere within the large boulder garden and completely out of sight from his rescuers. Tucking Kayden's helmet carefully under her arm, she started her hike upriver to where the rescue team was searching for him. Her feet flew over the boulders for the first one hundred yards, and her lungs burned as she scrambled over massive rock outcroppings still slick from the heavy rains that had only recently subsided. As she drew within earshot of the rescue team, Jenny yelled to her friends and lifted the helmet over her head. Will saw Jenny coming toward them and pointed in her direction. As she neared the group, Will, David, Reid, and Jo ran to meet her on a flat rock only a few feet from the river. It was not immediately clear whether this was good news or confirmation of Kayden's death.

As Jenny approached her friends, she could barely speak. The words that came from her mouth were unmistakable: "Kayden is alive!" she said, pointing to the message on the back of his helmet.

Four simple letters. She collapsed on the rocks, and tears flowed down her cheeks as she tried to catch her breath.

Jenny's next words were unexpected, alarming, and shocking to the team.

"Mark is gone. He . . ." She began to sob uncontrollably and was unable to finish.

Jo approached Jenny and put her arms around her. "Deep breathing, Jenny," she said. "What happened?"

After three deep breaths, Jenny spoke slowly with a quivering voice: "Mark and I encountered a mother bear and her cubs as we neared the top of the ridge. It was awful. We did not mean to come between them; it just happened. The mother bear was on the left side of the trail, and her cubs were on the right side. We came between them, the worst place to be." Jenny paused for a moment, staring into the clearing clouds in the distance. "The mother bear charged us. Mark held his ground, and he told me to make a break for the summit and call 911. As I ran toward the ridge, the bear attacked Mark. It was as if I was in a nightmare! I can't get the sight and sound out of my mind. The bear's claws tore into Mark's body. There was blood everywhere. There is no way he could have survived that attack."

The group stood in stunned silence and shook their heads in disbelief. The harsh reality set in as the team worried that neither Kayden nor Mark would be found alive. Slowly, David reached down, picked up Kayden's helmet, and ran his fingers over the roughly etched letters. The message of Kayden's survival was obvious and reenergized the entire rescue team. The sudden return of hope motivated them to make a final, all-out effort to locate and save him.

Chapter 14

*"In the depths of winter, I finally learned
there was an invincible summer."*

—Albert Camus

K ayden held the silver survival blanket tightly around his
body as he shivered and his teeth began to chatter. No matter how tightly he held the blanket, he could not get warm.
His situation remained critical, but for the first time he was able
to recognize a tangible improvement. The water was now leaving
the cave quicker than it was entering, and he expected it would
continue. He hoped his battle to breathe was over.

Kayden was fully aware that he was facing a new nemesis: crip-
pling cold. His shivering body and trembling hands were clear
signs of hypothermia. He struggled to strike the next match,
his hands shaking as he attempted to slide it against the striking
plate. Kayden had learned the basics of hypothermia in his first
whitewater-paddling clinic. He checked off the symptoms in his
mind: shivering, slurred speech, confusion, clumsiness, and poor
coordination. In his class, Will had said that children and teenagers

lose heat at a faster rate than adults, mainly because they have less body fat. Kayden was lean and muscular for his age. His two years of wrestling had transformed his body; he was very fit.

Kayden did not know exactly how long he had been in the cavern but knew it had been hours. How much time had passed? Was it dark outside now? He hoped not, since that would make rescue efforts more difficult, if not impossible. As the symptoms of hypothermia became more evident, Kayden tried to remember how to treat the condition. A cold fog had descended in his mind, slowing his ability to reason and sequence events, past and present. What could he do? Exactly how did he end up trapped in a dark cave on the verge of drowning? He could not remember. Another wave of panic began to build from within him, a familiar sense of dread that he had battled since first being forced under the rock at Hell's Gate. The cold was taking over his body and mind; he had to fight back! He took three deep breaths, slowly exhaling each time.

HELP. The word he had etched into his helmet entered Kayden's mind. Why? As those letters appeared in his thoughts, he slowly began to remember. He saw dashes between the letters. The dashed version was familiar; he had seen it before. The image emerged from the deep recesses of his memory. The acronym H–E–L–P had been written on the whiteboard during his paddling clinic to represent a strategy for minimizing hypothermia. Kayden had learned to use acronyms to remember important information.

HELP: Heat Escape Lessening Position. Kayden recalled the way to minimize heat loss by holding your knees close to your chest and forming a protective ball. This position had been impossible when Kayden had been stretching his body to obtain air; his desire to breathe had taken priority over everything. With the water now gradually leaving the cave, he moved his body slowly against the wall, using his torso to search for the perfect indentation that would allow him to sit in the HELP position. Even with his wetsuit and emergency blanket on him, Kayden knew the cold was hurting his ability to move and think. He longed for warmth. Although he was unable to see his lips, he was sure they had turned blue. Kayden had overcome many challenges throughout the afternoon. He remained determined not to surrender to the numbing cold water that entrapped him.

As Kayden rested in his heat-retaining position, he considered his options. He knew the water level was dropping. The sounds of cascading water seemed to have diminished, or was it his mind playing tricks on him? He hugged his knees harder, trying to retain every bit of heat he could as the cold water continued to lower his core body temperature. His muscular frame and minimal body fat offered little protection from the frigid waters of the Opa River.

The dreaded option again entered Kayden's mind. Was his best hope of escape to launch his body into the vortex and attempt to ride the powerful downward currents to safety? Was this even possible? Could he really save himself from a cold, dark death deep within the cavern? The icy water was penetrating every inch of his body and his tremors were increasing. He was unsure how long a person with hypothermia could survive. He knew an extremely low body temperature could kill him. How long did he have? He knew a person suffering from hypothermia would lose consciousness at some point, and his time was fast approaching. Once this occurred, Kayden would have to rely solely on the efforts of others to save him. He shivered again, prompted this time not only by the cold water but also by fear surging through his bewildered mind.

Kayden knew the hypothermia was taking its toll. As his options blurred, he reached for his matches. Light, any light, would be reassuring and allow him to evaluate any way out he might have missed. His hand shook more aggressively than before as he retrieved the canister. He slowly twisted the cap off, careful not to allow water to drip inside. He held the striking plate still and pushed hard against it with the wood match. No spark. His hands were shaking relentlessly, and it was difficult to hold the match steady. On his fourth attempt, the smell of sulfur filled his nostrils as the match lit up the cave. He scanned his environment, searching for anything he could use to help himself. He looked up and noticed that the ceiling of the cavern was higher than before! The water had dropped far faster than he'd thought possible. How had this happened? River levels change and typically increase and decrease over many hours. The water level had dropped more than two feet in what seemed a short amount of time, revealing a small sandy beach, barely visible as the water lapped against the slowly emerging shore.

Kayden was stunned at his good fortune! He could not believe his eyes and slowly slid his body in the direction of the spit of sand, ever mindful to keep the precious match case in his hand. As he slid onto the shore, he decided to use another match to explore his surroundings. Aside from the illuminating glow, the match cast a fleeting bit of warmth toward his hands. As the light pierced the darkness, Kayden saw the waterfall he had careened over. He could not believe he had survived the fall.

The light dimmed as the fire moved slowly down the match. Kayden continued to scan his surroundings, searching for any way to escape. His eyes darted about, his gaze probing ever deeper into the darkness. His eyes were looking straight up when he first saw it: a flicker of light, a small break in the blackness. A thin beam of light had appeared, just above the waterfall, dull and barely visible. Kayden's eyes fixated on the dim beam of light. Was it real or a visual hallucination? Had the intense glow of the match caused an aura in his vision? He remained transfixed on the light, growing slowly brighter above the waterfall. Kayden's body shook and his mind drifted. He shifted to his knees and began to crawl toward the beam, a thin ray of light piercing the darkness! He looked up and stared, watching it grow brighter by the second, as his hands and knees buckled beneath him. His head collapsed into the sand, and his body fell limp. Kayden's breathing slowed as the air slowly escaped from his blue lips. His eyelids closed and his body remained motionless. He had nothing left to give.

Chapter 15

*"Sometimes when you're in a dark place, you think you've
been buried, but you've really been planted."*

—Christine Caine

J enny's unexpected arrival from the summit of the mountain
provided mixed messages to the team members. Mark had
been mauled by an angry black bear on top of a nearby ridge.
His injuries had been severe and likely ended his life. Jenny had
witnessed the attack and could hardly speak about what she saw.
But she could not think about that right now. Kayden was still
alive, for now. The team members had to act quickly if they were
to save him.

Will, Reid, David, and Jo had carefully examined where
Kayden entered the Room of Doom and tried to track the flow
of the water. The powerful rush of water pulsing under the boulder had been reduced to a gentle stream. The improvised dam had
created an opening to the cavern four feet by three feet wide, large
enough for the team members to enter. The opening was both
inviting and intimidating, opposite qualities with a paralyzing

nature. Kayden's life hung in the balance. Sure, the cavern was accessible, but the risks were clear. If the kayaks used to construct the dam shifted, or had a structural failure, the full flow of the Opa River would resume with deadly consequences. Water would flood the underwater cave, drowning everyone in its path.

Will and Reid studied every detail to the entrance. Did they dare enter? The question was clear, the answer more elusive. Would the makeshift dam continue to hold the powerful waters at bay? Will and Reid beckoned for David, Jenny, and Jo to join them at the ledge just above the spot where the kayaks had been placed to create the barrier. Will and Reid were relieved to see the kayaks appeared stable. But were they? Occasional surges in the flow of the river would cause the kayaks to wobble, shifting hazardously up and down ever so slightly. When this occurred, the bow of the top kayak would nearly break the surface of the water. If this scenario worsened, the top kayak would likely be swept away, and their carefully constructed dam would collapse.

Will called the team together at the ledge. All options had been examined and everyone knew the dangers. Will's demeanor was serious and deliberate as he spoke. "Jenny made the 911 call, and a swift-water rescue team is on the way," he said. "We have two options: We can wait for the team to arrive and then enter the cavern to search for Kayden. Or we can go now and trust that our dam will hold."

Both plans had merit and could ultimately save or end Kayden's life. A brief and eerie silence settled over the group. Reid stepped away for one final look at their makeshift dam. He kneeled closer and stared at the two stacked kayaks under siege by the fast-moving currents. Reid returned to the group with determination on his face.

"The dam should hold," he said. "The time is now." Reid's expression conveyed a quiet confidence, and his tone was reassuring.

The other team members glanced at each other, uncertain who would speak next. Time stood still, and the constant sound of the cascading waters provided an unsettling backdrop as the group pondered their fate. David and Will surveyed their crudely constructed dam, and their gazes shifted toward each other. As their eyes met, their heads nodded in unison. No more waiting. Kayden was still alive, and time was short.

Reid addressed his rescue team. His message was clear and his tone confident. "Let's roll!" he said.

Jo and Jenny were assigned vital roles. They were to carefully monitor the dam. If anything changed, Jo was to let them know immediately by three loud blasts of her whistle into the cave. Jenny was to remain alert for the arrival of the swift-water rescue team by land or air. Their arrival was eagerly awaited and would provide an added measure of safety if something went wrong.

Reid, David, and Will gathered their rescue gear. David and Will were amazed at the items that emerged from Reid's bag. Rope, carabiners, and first aid kits are common items in a paddler's emergency kit. Harnesses and pulleys are less likely to be included, but Reid had packed these items at the last minute along with some other basic climbing gear. The steep ledges of the Opa River Gorge had captured his imagination on previous trips. Even a quick visit up a basic rock face would be a welcome addition to his day on the river. Reid also produced a small duffel that contained a sleeping bag liner and small headlamp. These items would be ideal if he were ever stranded by a river overnight. Will and David nodded at each other as these tools came out of Reid's survival bag.

The rescue team moved over the rocks to the entrance of the cavern. A final huddle was held to make sure all members of the team understood their roles. Reid would take point and secure a safety line as he entered the cave. Will and David were to maintain an interval of fifteen feet between them and keep one hand on the rope at all times. As Reid entered, he switched his headlamp to its brightest setting and scanned the cavern's walls, floor, and ceiling. The ceiling was higher than he'd expected. The walls were close but wide enough to walk in a straight line. The floor of the river was slippery, and the water moved faster than Reid had expected. The bank was also steeper than he'd realized. He carefully scanned the area directly in front of him. In the distance he heard an all-too-familiar sound: water tumbling over rocks. A waterfall loomed in the near distance as the group moved guardedly toward the cliff. David and Will had to follow Reid as his headlamp illuminated their path. The safety rope was reassuring, and each held the line tightly with one hand. As the roaring of the cascading waters grew closer, Reid stopped and held his hand high over his head, the beam of his headlamp trained on his clenched fist signaling the others to stop.

Will and David remained still as the beam of Reid's headlamp shifted from his clenched hand slowly toward the menacing sound of the waterfall. Reid was careful to make sure each step was deliberately planted in a secure spot on the river bottom. Any slip now would send him careening over the waterfall, likely bringing Will and David with him. He moved in his most surefooted manner, movements perfected by years of climbing on various rock surfaces. Will and David were thankful for his presence and expertise.

Reid's light moved ever closer to the sound of the waterfall. David's and Will's breathing increased as they moved closer to the edge of the waterfall. The rescue team stood transfixed as the beam suddenly stopped, motionless in the bowels of the Opa River. Reid's light suddenly shifted to the left, then right. This pattern repeated over and over as Reid searched the area below the water- fall for any sign of Kayden. On the fifth scan to the left, there, over by the wall, Reid caught his first glimpse of Kayden. He was lying face down, lifeless, on a small spit of sand. His body was cush- ioned from the beach by his bright yellow life jacket and silver survival blanket. Reid's heart sank as the beam of light illuminated Kayden's motionless body. He was awestruck by the strong swirl- ing currents of the water, twelve feet from Kayden's body. The waters spun in a perfectly circular pattern and then disappeared into the most powerful vortex Reid had ever seen. An ominous gurgling sound emerged from the center of the whirlpool as the waters spiraled downward with enormous power. Reid scanned the circling water with his headlamp and felt his stomach tighten. He turned the light away from the menacing vortex and directed it toward David and Will, mindful not to cast the beam directly into their eyes.

"I see him!" Reid's tone conveyed a sense of excitement and concern at the same time. The light from Reid's headlamp moved quickly as he retreated from the waterfall and toward his new friends. As they huddled in the dark, all three knew what was at stake. There would likely be only one chance for a rescue, and planning was critical. One slip, one mistake, and everyone would likely die inside the cold, dark cavern. If the makeshift dam failed, the waters of the Opa River would rapidly fill the cave; Kayden and all the members of his rescue team would be lost. Reid explained in concise detail the obstacles that lay before them. He would need to descend a twelve-foot waterfall to reach Kayden.

More alarming was the potentially lethal vortex, the deadly whirl-pool swirling all too close to Kayden's motionless body. Their plan had to be spot-on, and each member of the team had to execute their role. There would be no room for error.

An experienced climber, Reid was confident he could use his emergency gear to lift Kayden over the vortex and up the water-fall. The next step would be to transport Kayden out of the cavern as quickly as possible. The plan could be modified as needed, depending on the extent of Kayden's injuries. Reid feared Kayden would be unconscious and unable to help. Worse yet, he could have spinal or internal injuries. After creating the plan in his head, Reid explained it to David and Will, step by step.

"The first step is to set up a pulley system to lift Kayden over the vortex and up the waterfall," Reid said as he removed pulleys, harnesses, varied lengths of rope, and carabiners from his climbing bag. He wrapped a long rope around a boulder that would serve as the anchor to his rescue system. A small pulley was attached near the boulder to provide the mechanical advan-tage needed to lift Kayden's body up the waterfall.

Reid secured the rope to the boulder to descend the waterfall. The rope would be attached to a harness around his waist. After descending the waterfall, he would have to find a way to reach Kayden. The cavern walls were vertical, and water droplets made them very slippery. Avoiding the vortex was crucial. Reid knew it would be difficult to find the small cracks and ledges needed for his feet and hands to cross the wall and reach Kayden.

David and Will had a critical role in helping Reid reach Kayden. The safety line had to remain tight! If the line slipped, Reid could be pulled into the vortex. He emphasized the impor-tance of maintaining gentle pressure on the rescue line. He needed enough tension to avoid being drawn into the whirlpool without impairing his ability to maneuver. Once Reid reached Kayden, he planned to assess his condition before deciding how to best extract him from the cave. Ultimately, a harness would be used to secure Kayden and lift him over the vortex and up the waterfall.

The rescue plan was simple, in theory. Will, Reid, and David understood their roles. Reid would take the light with him, leaving David and Will to manage their tasks in near total darkness. Both gripped the rescue line with vise-like intensity. As Reid went over the waterfall, the beam of light moved in distinct arcs, all around the cavern. Reid's rescue bag with the harness and sleeping bag liner was strapped tightly on his back. As he neared the bottom of the cavern, Reid shined the light on the rock wall, searching for indentations, anywhere he could find traction. The walls were slick, and water dripped from the ceiling. He used his hands and feet to find the small crevices that allowed his body to adhere to the side of the walls. Reid slowly began moving in Kayden's direction.

The gurgling and popping sounds arising from the vortex startled Reid. He had never heard a sound like that before. After slowly inching along the walls of the cavern, he worked his body into a favorable position six feet above Kayden's body. Reid's path along the wall had been risky and his approach left him higher than he wanted. Could he jump? If Reid misjudged his landing from the wall, the consequences could be dire. He certainly did not want to land on Kayden, or stumble and be drawn into the vortex!

Reid's leg muscles burned, and his forearms ached from traversing the wall. He took three deep breaths. As he exhaled the third time, he pushed away from the wall. His descent was rapid, and he landed only feet from Kayden's head. He kneeled by Kayden's body and assessed his condition. Reid was well versed in emergency medical procedures, and recalled the acronym needed to assist victims.

ABCDE. Check Kayden's **A**irway, **B**reathing, **C**irculation, **D**isability, and **E**xposure. Reid looked for any sign of breathing and could see Kayden's chest movement was barely visible. He held his hand near Kayden's nostrils and was relieved to feel air moving ever so slightly. Kayden's lips were blue, an obvious sign of poor circulation and hypothermia. Reid was unsure of any other injuries. Kayden had obviously fallen over a waterfall and may have sustained severe internal injuries. He had been exposed to the cold waters of the Opa River for more than six hours. Even with a wetsuit, this type of exposure was often deadly. His overall condition was poor, and Reid knew a rapid extraction was needed if Kayden were to have any chance of survival.

Reid slipped off his small backpack and removed his sleeping bag liner and harness. Kayden was suffering from severe hypo-thermia and could not afford to lose any more of his body heat. Reid retrieved the liner from its stuff sack and rolled it out next to Kayden. He placed the liner at Kayden's feet and pulled it gently over his torso until his feet were flush against the bottom of the bag; this would help retain Kayden's remaining body heat. Next, Reid slipped the harness over Kayden's feet and secured it tightly around his waist. He was careful not to forget any import-ant details.

Once the harness and blanket were secured, Reid would guide Kayden's body as he was pulled over the vortex and up the right side of the waterfall. Once Kayden arrived in a safe spot at the top of the waterfall, the safety line would be lowered again for Reid to be hoisted up the waterfall. The extractions were the most danger-ous part of their plan. Reid was relieved to find the line remained taut as he readied Kayden's body to be pulled up the waterfall.

"Ready!" On the agreed-upon count of three, Reid lifted Kayden's body to the standing position as David and Will pulled with all their strength. Kayden's head hung loosely as his knees brushed the surface of the vortex before ascending quickly up the twelve-foot waterfall. Reid breathed a sigh of relief as he kept the beam of his headlamp trained on Kayden's limp body. Kayden had moved up the waterfall faster than Reid thought possible. His pulley system had worked to perfection! Will grabbed Kayden's motionless body and laid him flat on a smooth rock. Kayden's brisk ascent had required remarkable timing and cooperation; Reid breathed a sigh of relief as he waited for the rope to return.

Reid shined his headlamp near the top of the waterfall and saw David appear, rope coiled in his hands. Reid diverted the beam of light from the waterfall to a space on the sandy beach directly in front of him. As he trained his headlamp on the spot, a force struck him from above. Reid reeled from the impact as the object slithered down his shoulder. David's throw had been precise, and Reid clipped the rope to his harness and began the ascent out of the cavern. David and Will kept a constant pressure on the line as Reid was lifted briskly up the waterfall. After a fifteen-second ascent up the rock wall, he was reunited with Will, David, and Kayden. It was time to execute a hasty exit from the cave. Mission completed. Or was it?

Chapter 16

"I am prepared for the worst but hope for the best."

—Benjamin Disraeli

Jo and Jenny were unsure how long it had been since Reid, David, and Will had entered the cave. It seemed like an eternity. Jenny stood atop a large boulder, her eyes scanning the distance for any sign of a rescue team. Jo diverted her gaze from the entrance of the cavern to the two kayaks stacked dangerously on top of each other. The piled kayaks had been positioned perfectly, and Jo's confidence in the dam had increased. As she studied the structure, another positive sign developed. The water level on the river was dropping, at least by a few inches. This meant less pressure on the makeshift dam. She marveled as the waters slammed into the angled decks of the kayaks, changing the course of the water abruptly to the left and channeling over a four-foot waterfall.

Jo shifted her gaze from the dam back to the entrance of the cave. The safety of the rescue team required her to be vigilant. She frequently scanned the entrance to the rapid, including the precise spot where Mark had jumped onto the back of Kayden's kayak. Mark's careless act had initiated a series of catastrophic events, most notably Kayden's disappearance. Jo wondered about Mark's condition. The bear attack sounded horrible, and she knew Mark's chances of survival were unlikely. She glanced toward the ridge tops in the distance, wondering if Mark's lifeless body was somewhere up there. Her stomach tightened at the thought.

As Jo checked her surroundings, her mind drifted momentarily as the events of the day replayed in her mind. The trip had started smoothly with everyone in good spirits. Kayden had enjoyed meeting her father during the ride to the put-in. Somehow, that seemed long ago. She recalled a minor concern with Mark's presence on the river due to his reputation. He did not listen well to Will during the pre-trip briefing and seemed unfocused. However, Jo had a big heart and had believed that Mark would benefit from a river trip. Paddlers were, by nature, an accomplished and resilient group. Jo also believed that water had a healing effect on many people, and that Mark would be no different.

Jo redirected her focus to the job at hand. She had to keep a careful eye on the river for anything that might endanger the rescue team. Rivers reach their highest levels in the spring due to the frequent rains. As a result, it is not uncommon for debris from the riverbanks to wash directly into the river. This creates a variety of hazards for paddlers, most notably strainers. These are formed when large objects such as trees, logs, and branches are pinned against objects including rock ledges, bridges, and large boulders. The force of the moving water can entrap a kayaker, making escape impossible.

As she shifted her gaze upriver, her heart froze at the sight of an oncoming log entering the beginning of the rapid. It was the perfect size to destroy the dam and was bobbing up and down in the fast-moving waves. A T-shaped branch extended skyward from the middle of the log, helping Jo estimate the speed at which it was closing in on the dam. She estimated the wood to be about eight feet long, slightly shorter than their kayaks. It reminded Jo of a ram, like the kind the police used to break down doors. It was positioned in the center of the entrance rapid and gaining speed at an alarming rate. The stout wooden trunk was free flowing but appeared to be guiding itself with deadly accuracy toward the center of the makeshift dam.

Jo's mind raced with possibilities. Could she stop, or at least divert, the log? Would it be better to warn the rescue team the dam was about to fail? There was little time to ponder her options. The team's rescue efforts were about to take a dark turn that would place everyone in extreme danger. After surveying the size and speed of the log racing toward the two stacked kayaks, she concluded she had no means to prevent it from striking the dam. Jo estimated she could be at the entrance to the cavern to warn her friends in about fifteen seconds—if she acted now!

At a minimum, Jo could shout a warning deep into the cave, and the rescue team might have time to escape. She sprinted down the small rock ledges between her position and the entrance to the cavern. As she arrived at her destination, she reached for the whistle from her life jacket, placed it in her mouth, and blew with all her might. Three loud blasts on the whistle echoed into the cavern, a universal sign of danger. Surely, her friends would hear her warnings. She yelled deep into the recesses of the cave: "Get out now! The dam is about to break."

As Jo moved her body away from the entrance, she shifted her gaze in the direction of the dam. The log was gaining speed. Jo estimated that it would strike the makeshift dam dead center, dis-lodge the kayaks, and release a torrent of water back into the cave. She gasped as the log slammed into the top of the dam. The sound of impact was louder than she had expected. The top kayak folded in half and was swept into the entrance of the cave. The mangled mass of plastic was carried atop a powerful ribbon of turbulent water as it hurtled into the mouth of the cave directly toward the rescuers! The second kayak remained in place—for now. Jo stood motionless, and her heart sank.

Chapter 17

"H.O.P.E. = Hold On Pain Ends"

—Author Unknown

The alarming shriek of the whistle pierced the darkness and echoed through the cave, followed by two more. Jo was sounding the alarm! There was a clear and imminent danger. The team members moved as quickly as they could. Reid led the way with his headlamp as Will and David carried Kayden. Their escape route was not easy due to the narrow walls and low-hanging ceiling. At times, Will and David had to adjust how they carried Kayden's limp body. At the beginning of the trek out of the cave, Kayden was held up on each side by Will and David, the rescuers serving as human crutches to support Kayden's unconscious body. Transporting an unresponsive, 115-pound boy proved more challenging than they'd expected. Will's and David's backs throbbed as they stooped and struggled to maintain balance beneath the cave's low ceiling.

As Reid heard the repeated whistle blasts, he immediately closed the distance to rejoin Will and David. As he struggled to catch his breath, his tone was deadly serious.

"The whistle. Jo knows to use it only if there is extreme danger coming our way," he said. "We need to get out of here now!"

There was no time or need for discussion. Will turned his body and started in the direction of the exit from the cave. Reid and David followed as closely as possible, their labored breathing echoing off the walls in the cave. They were unsure of how far it was to the exit. A small circle of light loomed in the distance, marking their departure. It appeared close yet far away. It was difficult to determine the precise distance—maybe fifty feet?

The path was more difficult on the way out for one simple reason: gravity had befriended them on the way in but worked against them now. Will and David had to shift Kayden's body sideways to pass through two constricted passageways. This slowed their pace and required tremendous effort. Worse yet, they had difficulty breathing in the mist-filled cavern, the spray mixing with air as it entered their lungs. Kayden's body seemed to grow heavier with each step, and his breathing remained shallow, barely detectable.

As the group approached the narrowest part of their escape route, Reid raised his hand and closed his fist, signaling for his partners to stop. His voice was firm. "Listen! Do you hear it?" Reid asked. The sound was unmistakable, and his heart skipped a beat. Please no! They had come so far and were on the verge of successfully rescuing Kayden. This could not happen, not now! He shined his light in the direction of the sound, fear gripping his mind. As the light pierced the darkness, the nature of the emergency became clear. The group peered into the tunnel of light created by Reid's headlamp. Their eyes detected what they feared most: A large red object, bent into a V shape, was plowing toward them, being pushed by a cresting wave of water. The dam had failed, but how? It did not matter. The red kayak had been bent in half and was plummeting toward them. It had broken free from the dam; the waters of the Opa River and the kayak were heading for them fast! Their escape route was compromised, and the rescuers had little time to respond. The water was closing in, and Reid estimated that they had twenty seconds or less before it battered his team.

It was clear the red kayak had surrendered to the forces of the river. What about the other kayak, the blue one? Was it still diverting some of the water away from the entrance to the cave? If it held, they might still have a chance to escape. Reid kept his eyes trained on the frothy ribbon of water pushing the red kayak in his direction. Was the blue kayak close behind? If so, the dam would have completely failed, and the full force of the river would soon be channeled in their direction—with deadly consequences. Reid held his breath, fully expecting the blue kayak to appear at any moment. Time was running out for his team.

"Now!" Reid shouted. "We have to get out of here right now!" His tone of voice was undeniable, firm, and intense. "Move it! Do not let go of the rope or Kayden!" Will and David gripped the rope as tightly as possible with one hand and clung to Kayden with their other hand. The bent kayak was hurtling toward them half submerged! A moving kayak filled with water is a dangerous weapon that can crush a person upon impact.

Reid launched his body to one side of the cavern and braced his feet on a nearby boulder, ready to shove the boat out of harm's way. Timing was critical. When the boat drew near, he planted his arms on the deck of the kayak and pushed with all his might! The red V-shaped missile moved to the side, scraping by David and Will as they clung to Kayden. A direct hit would have knocked everyone down and swept them back over the waterfall.

With half of their makeshift dam now destroyed, the water level rose. The team members continued to lean forward and move their feet, battling against the strength of the waist-high waters. Progress was slow, painfully slow. Each step required considerable effort as they carefully planted their feet along the slippery floor of the cavern. One slip and the force of the river would take them back into the bowels of the cave with horrific consequences. The thought of plummeting over the waterfall and into the vortex was a terrifying possibility that sent a shiver through each member of the rescue team.

Slowly, the light at the entrance to the cave grew larger and began to illuminate their path out. The rushing water entering the cave remained at waist level, sometimes surging toward their chests. Each step was difficult and potentially their last. Reid was relieved he could see the exit. A pattern emerged as Reid led his team toward the light. He would turn his headlamp frequently toward his team members, making sure light was shed on the safest areas along their escape route.

The last twenty yards were the most difficult, and treacherous. Their escape route was steeper near the exit to the cave, resulting in water moving faster against their legs and waist. The force of the water tried to drive them back. Each member of the rescue team was exhausted, mentally and physically. Each step was more painful than the previous one. The sounds and smells of the cavern intensified as their hearts pounded in their chests. The team was close. So very close.

Will and David somehow quickened their pace for the final ten yards as Kayden's feet slithered over the final remaining boulders marking the exit from the cavern. Reid sprinted the final distance toward Jo and Jenny, their faces dark with worry. The sight of

the rescue team emerging from the cavern carrying Kayden overwhelmed Jo and Jenny. Was he alive? Kayden's body was limp and
his face ashen gray. The team members huddled over Kayden as he
was eased down on a large flat boulder near the river. Jo kneeled
by his side and placed her ears by his mouth. Tears streamed down
her cheeks as she heard the slow but unmistakable sound of air
escaping from his nostrils. Jenny wept. Kayden was alive.

Chapter 18

"Resiliency—when you bend in the wind
but don't break in the storm."

—Author Unknown

The sound was familiar and very welcome—it was the rapid staccato of rotors cutting through air. As the group huddled over Kayden at the entrance to the cavern, Reid scanned the mountaintops to the west and saw the first one flying low and fast. The sound drew closer, and he was pleased to see that three helicopters had crested the ridges of the mountains to the west of the Opa River Gorge. The lead chopper was moving directly toward them, while the other two hovered several thousand feet above. Life Flight was clearly emblazoned on the fuselages of two of the flying ambulances. The third helicopter was from a local news station.

The lead helicopter swooped toward the kayakers' location. As it drew closer, the pilot hovered, searching for a landing spot. The area was densely forested, and landing the chopper would be impossible. Will and Reid ran to a nearby boulder and scrambled to the top. Each began to wave their arms frantically to gain the attention of the pilot.

The lead pilot had flown helicopters in Afghanistan and was unfazed by the difficult mountainous terrain. He maneuvered his chopper in their direction, approaching at a speed that alarmed Will and Reid. In a moment, he was directly overhead and descended to an altitude of one hundred feet. The downward blasts of air from the rotors struck the rescue team with surprising force, and Jo huddled closely over Kayden to ensure that he was not blown into the river. The side door slid open, and a man in a flight suit appeared, his face clearly visible from below. Reid met his eyes and pointed urgently toward Kayden's prostrate body a few feet away. A rescue basket attached to a hoisting winch appeared from inside the helicopter. The crew stood at the open door as the basket was lowered, swinging in the slow arcs from the rotor wash above, and landed a mere ten feet from Kayden. Reid grabbed the side handles and moved the rescue basket next to Kayden's body. Carefully, Will lifted Kayden's head and shoulders while Reid guided the boy's legs and feet into the basket. They secured the basket's wide safety strap around Kayden's waist.

Will and Reid stepped back to allow the Life Flight paramedic and nurse to complete the evacuation. Will gave the thumbs-up sign, and the winch hoisted the basket to the open door of the helicopter. The basket was quickly drawn inside and cinched in place. The nose of the helicopter tilted forward as the pilot engaged the throttle of the powerful gas turbine. The downward rush of air generated by the blades hit the trees with the ferocity of a tornado, bending their trunks and branches toward the ground. The helicopter vanished over the mountain ridge as quickly as it had appeared.

Inside the chopper, the medical crew assessed Kayden's condition. He was breathing, but his respiration and heartbeat were extremely weak. His core body temperature was critically low, and he was unresponsive. The flight crew's assessment, "very critical," was not what the pilot wanted to hear. With no hesitation, the pilot reached for the throttle and pushed it all the way forward. The whine of the turbine increased, and the helicopter surged ahead, accelerating to its maximum speed of 160 miles per hour. The trauma team had forty-five minutes to prepare for Kayden's arrival—if he survived the flight.

The second air ambulance hovered in the distance, just above a mountain ridge two miles from Kayden's rescue team. Will, Jo, Jenny, and David peered into the distance as a paramedic and a rescue basket were lowered to the ridge top.

"Mark, they found Mark!" Jenny exclaimed. "That is close to where we were when the mama bear attacked." In an odd twist of fate, Mark had saved her life and nearly killed Kayden, all in the same day.

The others were shocked at Jenny's account of the gruesome bear attack Mark endured. He had sacrificed himself so Jenny could escape and hopefully save Kayden's life. This selfless act required bravery and was a testament to Mark's true character. He had made a fateful mistake on the river that put everyone on the trip in jeopardy, especially Kayden.

Mark, like everyone on the trip, was complicated. He had encountered hardship and heartbreak in his life. His tough and callous demeanor did not reflect who he truly was. He had stepped forward and saved Jenny's life, an unselfish response that helped everyone see him in a new light.

The group stood in stunned silence as they watched the basket that held Mark being hoisted skyward with the paramedic suspended from the cable. Both were retrieved by the flight team at the helicopter door. The door closed, and the familiar whine of the gas turbine reverberated throughout the valley as the helicopter accelerated to maximum speed.

The trauma center was 120 miles away. The triage team was ready and awaiting the arrival of two teenagers in critical condition. The flight paramedics had been candid in their evaluation of both victims. Kayden was in an advanced stage of hypothermia. His vital signs were very weak. His face was ashen, and he was unresponsive. Mark had sustained severe lacerations to his back, neck, arms, and legs. He had lost nearly half the blood in his body and was unconscious when they rescued him. As the doctors and nurses prepared for their arrival, they knew Kayden's and Mark's chances of survival were slim.

Chapter 19

"Use pain as a stepping stone, not a campground."

—Alan Cohen

After landing on the roof of the trauma center, Kayden and Mark were whisked away to separate triage rooms for assessment. Kayden was near death. His trauma team worked furiously to treat his life-threatening symptoms. An oxygen mask was placed over his mouth to feed warm, humid air into his lungs. His blood was very cold and would not circulate within his body. The medical team hooked Kayden up to a heart bypass machine to gradually rewarm his blood. Kayden's body was slow to react at first; the frigid waters of the Opa River had taken their toll.

Kayden remained unconscious for eight hours. When he slowly opened his eyes the next morning, he was unsure of his surroundings. His vision was blurry as he struggled to focus on the person next to him, grasping his still-cold hand.

Mrs. Barrett held Kayden's hand tightly and smiled lovingly at him. Tears rolled down her cheeks as she looked into her son's eyes. "Kayden, you made it," she said. "I am so proud of you."

Kayden squeezed his mom's hand tightly as she stared into his eyes. Kayden saw another person in the room, standing behind his mom. Large tears were also rolling down her cheeks as she approached his bed. He recognized Jenny immediately. She had been crying yet somehow still looked beautiful. Her mouth opened but no words came out. None were needed.

Jo, Will, David, and Reid were waiting outside, anxious to see Kayden and hear his voice. Their ordeal had been beyond anything they could have ever imagined. Kayden's last memory was of crawling across the small spit of sand in the cavern, moving his body in the direction of the light. As he heard the story of his rescue, tears welled up in his eyes. His heartfelt gratitude was evident as he thanked each of his rescuers for putting their lives on the line to save him. Kayden was exhausted from the previous day's ordeal, and hearing the events that led to his rescue added to his fatigue. His eyes gently closed, and he fell asleep until noon when his nurse arrived with his lunch.

Kayden had not eaten in more than forty-eight hours, and the bacon, lettuce, and tomato sandwich on his plate was the best he had ever tasted, even if it was hospital food. The french fries were also perfect, crispy, and fried to a golden brown. As he finished the last one, he heard another knock on the door. Kayden's eyes widened as Dr. Johnson and Mrs. McGhee entered the room with cards in their hands. They had heard of Kayden's rescue and came to the hospital to check on him. Both wore large smiles as they approached his bed.

"Well, Kayden, you gave us quite a scare. You have no idea how glad we are to see you!" said Mrs. McGhee, her voice trailing off as tears flowed down the side of her face.

Dr. Johnson spoke next: "Kayden, word of your accident traveled fast, and you have more visitors in the hallway who want to see you. Our entire group showed up thirty minutes ago. They told me they aren't leaving until they see you. Are you okay with a few more visitors?"

Kayden's eyes blurred with tears, the good kind. He was moved by the support of his new friends. One by one, Beau, Jay, Laura, and Sarah entered the room, each holding a card and a balloon. Each of them sat gently alongside Kayden's hospital bed and gave him a hug. Cindy was the last to enter from the hallway. He was surprised and happy to see her. Her foster parents had brought her to the hospital at her insistence. She had been terribly upset when she learned of Kayden's disappearance and wanted to see her friend. Kayden was surprised and happy that each of his group members had made it to the hospital to see him. The bond that had developed in their group was special and strong. To Kayden, it felt like his second family had come to visit at just the right time.

After hearing of the accident, Mark's family rushed to the hospital to be there when he arrived. His trauma team had worked feverishly to stabilize him. He had suffered extensive injuries, including lacerations to the main arteries in his body. His condition went from bad to worse upon his arrival. During surgery, Mark's heart stopped, and the doctor had to use the defibrillator to restart it. The head trauma doctor had treated soldiers with severe combat wounds in Iraq, many of which paled in comparison to Mark's wounds. In a lifesaving move, Mark had assumed a defensive position when the bear attacked. He'd clasped his hands over the back of his neck and huddled in a protective ball. The bear had slashed him with her claws for more than a minute. To Mark, the attack seemed to last an eternity.

After he spent three days in a medically induced coma, Mark's condition slowly improved, and his vital signs stabilized. His recovery was slow and tedious. His parents had been by his side the whole time, together for him. He had many visitors in the hospital. His spirits were lifted by visits from his classmates who heard his story. He also appreciated the many texts and social media posts wishing him a speedy recovery. David, Will, Reid, and Jo stopped by for regular visits. He looked forward to seeing Kayden and Jenny; he had his apology ready.

Mark had made a mistake, a costly one. He had also redeemed himself for his actions. His courage in the face of adversity was obvious. He had sacrificed himself to save Jenny and Kayden. Mark's view of the world had changed, and for the first time, he was proud of who he saw in the mirror.

After staying in the hospital for seven days, Mark was excited about going home. His family and friends had rallied at his bedside, and he was on the mend. He was still sore, and more than one hundred stitches remained in his body. As he stood slowly by his bed, he heard a knock on the door. When it opened, Mark was pleased to see Kayden and Jenny. They entered the room slowly, hand in hand, and approached Mark, unsure of what to say.

The events that transpired on the river that fateful day had been harrowing and nearly cost two lives. All three had time to think about their experiences, a process that would continue for the rest of their lives. They had responded to a series of mishaps and improvised with whatever resources they could find. The problems on the river trip had occurred without warning. To their credit, Kayden, Mark, and Jenny, with help from their friends, had found a way to adapt—to roll with the changes! They had endured one hardship after another and remained focused on helping each other. In the end, no words were needed as the trio embraced. It was over and they had survived.

Epilogue

> *"I am not what happened to me. I am what I choose to become."*
>
> —Carl Jung

Kayden's survival on the river was no accident. Even by the young age of twelve, Kayden's parents had prepared him for life's challenges. They cared for him deeply and made sure he was held accountable for his actions. Kayden always knew where his boundaries were, and he was taught to be respectful toward peers and adults. He never hesitated to talk to his parents, even about awkward and uncomfortable topics.

Many of Kayden's prior experiences were especially helpful when his life was in jeopardy on the Opa River. His scouting experiences taught him basic survival skills that were helpful in the cavern. His ability to remain calm and manage resources was critical to his making it out of the cave alive. His matches, whistle, helmet, blanket, and knife were key tools he used to his advantage.

Never give up. Kayden's dad and his wrestling coach had instilled this belief in him at an early age. He internalized the value of *never* giving up, even when situations appear hopeless.

This idea was also reinforced repeatedly by another positive role model in his life, his paddling instructor Will Sully. These three adults conveyed an undeniable truth. There is hope in *every* circumstance. Options may come disguised as hard work or require an unusual approach, but Kayden realized that outside-the-box solutions were fine and sometimes preferred. These three mentors helped Kayden benefit more than he ever realized. His experience in youth wrestling and paddling helped provide a strong foundation for building resiliency skills. As a result, Kayden's mental toughness, strength, endurance, coordination, and alertness were far more advanced than usual for a twelve-year-old.

Lessons learned from his time in Dr. Johnson and Mrs. McGhee's grief group sessions were also key to his survival. Although he hid it well, Kayden had been deeply hurt by his father's untimely death; he had often cried himself to sleep at night. He was convinced that no one could possibly understand the depth and breadth of his pain. He was shocked and encouraged to learn that he was not alone in his grief experience, that some of his friends had endured very painful life experiences as well. The concept of resiliency stuck in his heart and mind like glue and would make all the difference in his escape from the cave.

One axiom reinforced by Kayden's experience was the importance of having friends, good friends, individuals who could truly be counted on in times of trouble. He was most appreciative of his friends who came to his rescue that fateful day on the Opa River.

Kayden had learned that he was solely responsible for his actions—on the river and in life. Blaming others would not work. His behavior was his sole responsibility, and what he did (or did not do) each day *mattered*. His parents were supportive but never rescued him from his mistakes. He could still hear his dad's voice clear as day: "Kayden, how is that working for you?" His dad's expression was always the same when he offered this question. Kayden knew he had messed up, and it was time to try something different.

He had also learned the importance of attitude. Words were his most valuable tool. The words he chose and how he delivered them were powerful. He had been surprised to learn that attitude included words *and* body language. Although he was generally aware of his expressions and gestures, he was shocked to learn from his wrestling coach that he would sometimes roll his eyes and look away from adults. He was cautioned about this behavior and became more aware of how he used his words and body to connect with others.

Kayden's time in the cave helped him understand the power of optimism, even in the darkest of times. When the water was rising above his head, he maintained his belief that somehow he would survive. He yearned for the light of day, the warm sun, and the company of his friends. Somehow, he would find it.

Kayden's final takeaway was that resiliency included planning and setting goals. This became etched in his psyche. His main goal had been to avoid the vortex and somehow find a way to escape the terrifying circumstances he faced. Kayden was grateful for his life, and he longed to see Jenny and his mom again. His ability to plan and solve problems ultimately led to his decision to etch the message of HELP into his helmet and cast it into the vortex. This action eventually saved his life. His resilient nature became solidified on the tragic day he was trapped in the underwater cavern. His resiliency skills would remain with him for the rest of his life.

Kayden was surprised by the level of interest in his story. One of the helicopters that had arrived on the scene the day of the accident was a local news team, and Kayden was interviewed in the hospital about his ordeal. Several other network news organizations interviewed him and, later, Mark. The level of interest slowly waned over time, and by the time he was in eighth grade, the experience was seldom mentioned around his school.

Mark recovered from the wounds inflicted by the bear. His physical scars remained and were outward evidence of a teen who had sustained serious, life-threatening injuries. The scars slowly faded as he grew older but never disappeared. Mark's changes on the inside were greater. On the day the bear attacked him, Mark understood for the first time what it was like to be completely helpless to a force far more powerful than he. The lens through which he viewed the world changed, yielding a far more compassionate approach toward others. The change was evident to everyone who knew him.

At Kayden's urging, Mark joined the wrestling team and proved to be a natural at the sport. In his senior year, he was voted team captain by his teammates and became a regional champion in the 220-pound class. He was also elected vice president of the student council. His grades slowly improved through high school, and he was accepted to several universities during his senior year.

Kayden's dreams about the day his dad died became less frequent. Kayden continued to dream about his father, and not only about the day of his fatal accident. Sometimes the dreams were very real, and Kayden could see and talk to his dad. Kayden liked these dreams best. A flashback to his day on the Opa River also frequented his dreams. The events of that day would replay in his mind, and at times, he would awaken covered in sweat. The dream was consistent and always included the same people. It was not all bad. He liked seeing Jenny and his mom at his bedside in the hospital.

Kayden and Jenny remained good friends through middle school. They shared a bond no other middle-school student could imagine. Jenny's family moved when she was in high school, and Kayden and Jenny slowly drifted apart. After years of hard work in high school and a few academic challenges, Kayden was admitted to the University of North Georgia. During his freshman orientation, an attractive blonde woman entered the auditorium. She had a distinctive walk, and Kayden recognized Jenny immediately. Their eyes met from across the room, and their reconnection was immediate and strong. It did not take long for Kayden to ask her out to dinner.

On their first date, they walked to the Dahlonega town square and enjoyed dinner at an outdoor café. The umbrella lights cast a glow on Jenny's face as she nibbled on an appetizer. Jenny was a great conversationalist; she could somehow read Kayden's mind, his innermost thoughts and fears. They had a connection like no other. He reached for her hand across the table, and her hand met his halfway. When their hands touched, it was clear. Their connection was stronger than ever, and neither of them wanted to let go—ever.

The Adventure Continues

Learn from yesterday. Live for today.
Hope for tomorrow.

—Albert Einstein

PREREADING ACTIVITY

Into the Vortex is about resiliency, the ability to adapt and change in response to problems in your life. Make a list of the skills needed to overcome adversity in your life. Consider how your choice of friends, controlling your emotions, and decision making affect your own resiliency.

WRITING ACTIVITY: WHEN LIFE FLIPS YOU OVER, ROLL WITH THE CHANGES!

Kayden's story is unique. His experiences of losing his father and nearly drowning pushed him to his absolute physical and mental limits. Yet, he never considered quitting and remained an active problem solver. His core resiliency skills were essential to his survival. He kept friends close and assumed personal responsibility for his actions. He maintained a positive attitude in the face of adversity and retained an optimistic outlook. Kayden was a planner and set goals to mark his progress. In the end, these skills served him well. His takeaway in this story was that failure is not an option; no matter how dark the circumstances, there are *always options* to pursue.

- Create a resiliency tool kit for your life. What would you include?

- Write a paper that describes your most frightening experience. How did you respond? Include specific resiliency skills that helped you survive your ordeal.

DISCUSSION TOPICS

- What were the most important skills Kayden demonstrated to survive his circumstances?

- Make a list of three important decisions Kayden made that enabled him to survive his ordeal on the Opa River.

- What tools did Kayden utilize to aid in his survival? How were these beneficial?

- Describe one additional tool Kayden could have used in the cavern. How would it have helped him?

- In a technical sense, a vortex is a mass of wind or water that spins around fast and pulls objects down into its empty center. A vortex is also a powerful metaphor for dangerous situations. Describe dangerous influences in your life that may pull you down and cause problems in your life. What are these dangers? How can you avoid them?

- Kayden's dad encouraged him to participate in activities such as scouting, wrestling, and kayaking. How did this benefit Kayden?

- Name two adults who helped Kayden develop resiliency skills. Describe the skills Kayden learned and how they helped him survive his ordeal on the Opa River. How did these skills impact Kayden later in life?

- Kayden valued relationships. How did he treat others in his life? How did this help him?

- Kayden and Jenny had a special bond. How did their connection influence their behavior in the story?

- Kayden had to make a difficult choice: wait for others to help him or swim into the vortex. What would you have done in his situation? Explain your answer.

- Why do you think Kayden's search team never gave up on him?

- What did Mark learn from his mistakes in the story? How did this help him?

- Read the poem "Wreckage" by Nikita Gill on the last page of the book.

- "There is nothing beautiful about the wreckage of a human being." What does the first sentence mean to you?

- What resources would be available in your "ocean of courage" when facing a difficult situation?

- Describe a difficult time in your life (i.e., your wreckage) and how you were able to grow and learn from your experience. Include key people that helped support you during your time of need.

- Explain how you may have helped others overcome "wreckage" in their life. What did you do to support them?

- The definition of "wreckage" varies from person to person, life to life, as does "picking through" it. Why are some people more successful than others in the rebuilding?

About the Story

Many of the events in this story are true. My interest in resiliency emerged when I was in college after I had an accident in a kayak on the Meadow River in West Virginia in 1988 in which I nearly drowned. This river was well known for undercut rocks and dangerous hydraulics. The Opa River is fictitious but is based on my kayaking experiences on the Chattooga, Etowah, Nantahala, Ocoee, Nolichucky, French Broad, New, Gauley, and Meadow Rivers. I also survived a head-on collision with a drunk driver on a South Carolina interstate the following year. My initial interest in resiliency evolved into a passion that directly impacted how I served students as a school psychologist in the Cobb, Rockdale, and Cherokee County School Districts in Georgia for twenty-five years.

Into the Vortex: A Tale of Resiliency was inspired by an unusual series of events. In April of 2002, I married JoAnne Renfro, a special-education teacher with three children, ages four, nine, and twelve. Her husband, Kevin, was a friend of mine who had unexpectedly passed away in the year 2000. Kevin and JoAnne were remarkable parents who were loved by everyone in their community. Kevin was a fantastic father and husband; his sudden passing shocked everyone who knew him, most of all his parents, wife, children, and church family.

During the early years of our marriage, JoAnne and I saw first-hand how the loss of a father could impact the development of children. Many of the descriptions and reactions of grief our children experienced are embedded in Kayden's story. Our journey has not been easy, but it has been uniquely rewarding. We learned many important lessons on the way. Kalyn, Erica, and Kevin Carl ("K.C.") Renfro experienced adversity on their journey to adulthood. To their credit, they persevered and matured into resilient, loving, and insightful adults. Our ten-year-old grandson Kayden is also a resilient and insightful child; thus, the main character in the story is named after him.

As the saying goes, "Everyone has a story to tell." It is my hope that Kayden's tale of resiliency, based on real-life events, will inspire you to overcome whatever challenges or hardships you face in life. Do not allow yourself to be drawn into the vortex, whatever that might be for you.

For more information and resources about resiliency, please visit **www.ResilientHorizons.com**.

—John Poidevant

Wreckage

*There is nothing beautiful about the wreckage of a
human being. There is nothing pretty about damage,
about pain, about heartache. What is beautiful is
their strength, their resilience, their fortitude as they
display an ocean of courage when they pick through
the wreckage of their life to
build something beautiful brand new, against
every odd that is stacked against them.*

—Nikita Gill

About the Author

John Poidevant, PhD, currently serves as president of Resilient Horizons and provides resiliency training for youth and adults. He was previously the lead school psychologist with the Cherokee County School District. In 2013, the Georgia Association of School Psychology recognized him as the School Psychologist of the Year. Before this, John served as an assistant professor and coordinator of school counseling at the University of North Carolina at Greensboro. He was the founder and director of Developmental Associates, a quality provider of mental health training programs. John also has experience in the private sector, most recently with the Center for Psychological and Educational Assessment in Marietta, Georgia.

John's diverse professional history includes numerous publications in professional journals and magazines. An active speaker, his engaging and practical presentations have led to many opportunities to present at local, state, regional, national, and international conferences.

As the founder and president of Resilient Horizons, John has led an adventurous and challenging life. An avid kayaker, sailor, and motorcyclist, he continues to navigate the waters and roads of the southeast at every opportunity.

Manufactured by Amazon.ca
Bolton, ON